BUSINESS WITH PLEASURE

Lisa turned off the lights, came back with some pillows, and put them behind me. Then she shrugged off her bathrobe, lay down against me, and pulled the robe over both of us.

"Garret, what are you thinking?"

"I never killed anything before. I don't even hunt."

"Stop it. You had to do it."

"The worst part about killing him isn't that he's dead; he probably deserved worse. It's that I'm the one who did it. I know that I can kill. I don't like knowing that about myself."

She put her cheek against my shoulder and kissed me gently on the neck. I kissed her back, a long time, and put my arm around her. With my right hand I traced the line of her jaw. She closed her eyes and pressed her cheek against my palm. Then her left hand slid down my chest.

"You know," I said, "I've never done this with a client before. . . ."

THE
JANUARY
CORPSE

New from the #1 bestselling author of *Communion*—
a novel of psychological terror and demonic possession. . . .
"A triumph."—Peter Straub

UNHOLY
FIRE
Whitley Strieber

Father John Rafferty is a dedicated priest with only one
temptation—the beautiful young woman he has been counseling, and who is found brutally murdered in his Green-
wich Village church. He is forced to face his greatest test
of faith when the NYPD uncovers her sexually twisted
hidden life, and the church becomes the site for increas-
ingly violent acts. Father Rafferty knows he must over-
come his personal horror to unmask a murderer who
wears an angel's face. This chilling novel will hold you in
thrall as it explores the powerful forces of evil lurking
where we least expect them. "Gyrates with evil energy
. . . fascinating church intrigue."—*Kirkus Reviews*

THE
JANUARY
CORPSE

Neil Albert

AN ONYX BOOK

ONYX
Published by the Penguin Group
Penguin Books USA Inc., 375 Hudson Street,
New York, New York 10014, U.S.A.
Penguin Books Ltd, 27 Wrights Lane,
London W8 5TZ, England
Penguin Books Australia Ltd, Ringwood,
Victoria, Australia
Penguin Books Canada Ltd, 10 Alcorn Avenue,
Toronto, Ontario, Canada M4V 3B2
Penguin Books (N.Z.) Ltd, 182-190 Wairau Road,
Auckland 10, New Zealand

Penguin Books Ltd, Registered Offices:
Harmondsworth, Middlesex, England

Published by Onyx, an imprint of New American Library, a division of
Penguin Books USA Inc. This is an authorized reprint of a hardcover edi-
tion published by Walker Publishing Company, Inc.

First Onyx Printing, January, 1993
10 9 8 7 6 5 4 3 2 1

PUBLISHER'S NOTE
This is a work of fiction. Names, characters, places, and incidents either
are the product of the author's imagination or are used fictitiously, and any
resemblance to actual persons, living or dead, events, or locales is entirely
coincidental.

To DONALD E. DEIBLER
who never wavered. Never.

And to
JACK EBERSOLE
for all his help and
encouragement.
Thanks.

1

FRIDAY, 11:00 A.M.

I couldn't stand the sight of him, but I took his case anyway.

I'd been sitting in the spectator's section of a courtroom in the basement of the Court of Common Pleas of Philadelphia County. At night the room was used for criminal arraignments, and it showed. Everything in the room was dirty, even the air. When I breathed I could feel the grittiness of a factory or garage entering my lungs. The bare wooden benches were thickly carved in complex, overlapping swirls of graffiti, initials, gang emblems, and phone numbers. Some people called it street art. I didn't.

To my left, fifteen feet off the ground, a clock was built into the wall. It was missing its hands and most of the brass numerals, and the few that were left were muddy brown. Not that I cared too much what time it was; as long as I sat there, waiting to testify, my meter was running.

Today the room was being used by the Family Court for a custody case. This was the second day of trial, and the wife's attorney was hoping to get

me on the stand today. There's no such thing as a
custody case with class. The couple were both doctors. Married ten years; two children, both girls,
ages four and seven. Separated two years ago. Each
had a condo; his was just south of Society Hill in
a newly gentrified area; hers was on Rittenhouse
Square. They both had memberships at the usual
country clubs, plus time-shares in both Aspen and
Jamaica. She drove a BMW and he drove a Benz.

It had been amicable at first. Neither one was
leaving for someone else; they just didn't like being
married to each other anymore. And there was no
one stirring it up. Most spouses need encouragement to get really nasty—a new girlfriend, a
mother, a friend, or a lawyer. So it was very civi-
lized. For a while. Then, in the course of working
out a property settlement, her lawyer found that her
husband had forgotten to disclose his half-interest
in a fast-food franchise—a small matter of half a
million dollars. In response, she dropped the
blockbuster; she moved to terminate his visitation
rights because he was sexually abusing the seven-
year-old. He denied the charge and countered with
a suit for attorney's fees and punitive damages. The
case had started yesterday, was being tried again
today, and would probably be going on for a good
chunk of the next two weeks.

I had very little to say, but the wife's lawyer
wanted me to testify anyway. In a close case almost
anything might make a difference. I'd followed the
husband for a week, and the most interesting thing
I'd found was that he read *Penthouse*. Plus, as I
was sure his lawyer would point out on cross, *Time*,

Sports Illustrated, Business Week, and *The New England Journal of Medicine.*

The wife's attorney, sitting at counsel table, turned to me, pointed to his watch, and shook his head. The cross-examination of the wife's child psychologist was hopelessly bogged down on the question of her credentials, and they weren't going to reach me that day. The case wasn't on again until the following Wednesday; I was free till then. I nodded, pointed to my own watch to indicate that my meter was off and headed for the door. My overcoat was already over my arm; no one familiar with the Court of Common Pleas of Philadelphia County leaves their property unattended. There used to be a sign outside the public defender's office: *Watch your hat, ass, and overcoat.* Somebody stole it.

The corridor was as filthy as the courtroom, but at least there was light. And people—lots of them. The young and shabbily dressed ones were there for misdemeanor criminal or family law cases. The felony defendants were usually older and better dressed; they'd learned, usually the hard way, that making a good impression just might help. But the best dressed of all—except for the big-time drug defendants, who put everyone to shame—were the civil trial attorneys. There was big money in personal injury work and large commercial claims, and a lot of it was worn on their backs. My own suit, when it was new, had looked like theirs; now it was dated and worn, and my tie had a small stain. I tried to comfort myself that it was good enough for what I did now. It didn't help.

I was nearly to the exit, feeling blasts of cold air

as people went in and out, when I heard him calling
my name. The voice was raspy and nasal. I turned;
it was Mark Louchs, a classmate of mine from law
school. He practiced with a small firm out in the
suburbs. His hairline had receded since I'd last seen
him, and he was wearing new, thicker glasses. His
skin was red, probably from a recent Caribbean
vacation. He smiled, shook my hand, and said he
was so glad to see me. It was all too fast and too
hearty, and I didn't buy any of it. I hadn't liked
him back in law school, and nothing that had happened since had changed my view.

"Hello, Mark. Going well for you?"

"God, hearings coming out my ears. Clients
calling me at all hours. Can't get away from it. My
accountant—I'm busy as hell—" He stopped himself. "Yeah. Fine. Look, you know how badly I
feel about what happened to you." His voice trailed
off. He'd been a shit when I needed his help and
we both knew it. I said nothing, letting the awkward silence go on. It was a small revenge, watching him feel uncomfortable, but that didn't stop me
from enjoying it. When he was nervous, I noticed,
his smile was a little lopsided.

Finally he went on. "Look, I hear you're doing
investigations now?"

I nodded. "It's the closest thing I can do to keep
my hand in. And I'm sure not going to be a para-
legal."

"I tried to reach you first thing this morning.
They said you were out."

"Sitting all day in court, waiting to testify. I
haven't checked my messages yet."

"Listen, I'd like you to do me a favor. Are you set up to handle a rush job?"

I do plenty of favors, but not in business. And not for someone who didn't respond to my request for a letter of support when I'd gone before the disciplinary board with my license on the line. I kept my voice disinterested and cautious. It wasn't hard. "How much a favor and how much a rush?"

"An investigation for a case to be heard Monday at one-thirty."

I carefully gave a low whistle, watching for his reaction. "Gee, I don't know. That gives me just the rest of today and the weekend. Pretty short notice."

"If you can do it, the fee should be no problem. I'm sure we can agree on an acceptable rate."

I looked at his suit and at my own. I knew the money would never wind up in a suit; I had too many other bills. But it gave me something to focus on. I pursed my lips. "Well, let's go somewhere and hear about it."

We put on our overcoats, cut through the perpetual construction around City Hall and wound up at a small bar near Sansom and Sixteenth. He found a quiet corner booth and ordered two coffees, decaf. Whatever serious lawyers do after five, they don't drink during the day.

"Ever do a presumption of death hearing?" he asked.

"Fifteen years ago, fresh out of law school, I did a memo for a partner."

"Familiar with the law?"

"Unless it's changed. If all you have is a disappearance, no body or other direct proof of death, the passage of seven years without word gives rise to a presumption of death. If the person were alive, the law assumes that someone would have heard from them.''

''You're right; and the law hasn't changed. Here's what we've got. I represent the survivors of a man who disappeared under circumstances strongly suggestive of his death. Name of Daniel Wilson. We've filed an action to have him declared dead; our hearing is Monday afternoon at one-thirty in Norristown. There's a life insurance policy at issue, and the insurance company is going to fight tooth and nail.''

''What carrier? I do some work for USF & G and for Travelers. I'd hate to get on their bad side.''

''Neither of them. Some one-lung life insurance outfit out of Iowa. Reliant Fidelity Mutual, or something like that. I never heard of them before; I don't think they write any casualty or liability.''

''Let's hear some more.''

''He lived in Philly and had offices in the city and in Norristown. I figured that his office in Norristown gave me enough to get venue there. The insurance company didn't care, so that's where the hearing will be.''

''What kind of office did he have?''

''A law office. Never heard of the guy before this case, though. I made a couple calls to friends from law school, but neither of them knew him.''

''A lawyer who disappeared. This is starting to get interesting.''

''Wait till you hear about the disappearance. Just after New Year's, seven years ago. His sister is in town from LA; they plan to get together. Two separate cars. She finds his car off the road full of bullet holes. Blood, but no body. Police can't turn up shit. It's Powell Township, Berks County, by the way. Never heard from again.''

It was hard trying to keep the excitement out of my voice. It was short notice, but I had no plans for the weekend. It sounded like a break from skip traces and catching thieving employees. ''Well, sounds like a case I could handle for you. Who was involved before?''

Even in the dimness I could tell he was blushing. ''Yeah. You're right; you're getting sloppy seconds. The Shreiner Agency was handling it till yesterday afternoon.'' I just sat there until he decided to continue. ''They did the usual interviews, credit checks, asset checks, and so forth. Then they hand-delivered back the file with a check refunding all of their bills we had paid. And a letter saying they wouldn't be able to help any further. No reason.''

I was torn between my curiosity and my self-interest. ''Sounds like someone warned them off.''

''Oh?'' he said disingenuously. ''There could be any number of reasons, I suppose.''

''Have they returned your phone calls?''

He hung his head. ''No.''

''This thing smells to me. Like organized crime. That's out of my league.''

''Look, nobody's asking you to find who killed him—just to say that there's no evidence he's alive. That ought to be easy enough.'' He didn't say, even for you, but the words hung in the air.

''Tell that to the Shreiner Agency.''

He finished his coffee. He was anxious to get

help, but I was clearly hitting a nerve. "Yes or no?"

I normally worked for a flat fifty dollars an hour. Right then, considering who I'd be helping and what had happened to the Shreiner Agency, I didn't care if I got the case or not. "I charge my attorney's rate—one hundred fifty per hour, two hundred for work outside of business hours, half rate for travel time, plus all expenses."

It was his turn to whistle.

"Think you can come up with something for that kind of money?"

"Haven't the slightest idea. I work by time, not results."

"That's a lot of money."

"It's quarter to twelve, and it's Friday."

He gave me the kind of look I didn't normally associate with being hired—it was closer to the expression you see when you steal somebody's parking place. But he grunted something that sounded like "okay" and gave me his business card with his home number on it. And the Shreiner file—there was so little of it, he was carrying it in his breast pocket.

"I'll look this over and do what I can this afternoon. When can I meet the sister?" I asked.

"Give me your card. I'll have her at your office at nine tomorrow morning."

"Make it seven; I don't want to lose any time on Saturday. Some witnesses may be unavailable for interviews on Sunday."

"Okay, but keep me posted, will you? Remember that you're working under the supervision of an attorney."

"Right." I wanted to tell him that I was working under the supervision of an asshole, but I let it pass.

Philadelphia has fairly mild winters, but early January is no time to linger outside. I needed a quiet place to read. I headed east to Suburban Station, walked down a flight of stairs, and found an empty bench.

The Shreiner Agency was like the Army: bloated, bureaucratic, and sluggish, and most of its best people moved along after a few years. Yet they were careful and scrupulously honest. That counted for a lot in my business.

When I unfolded the file, I found it was only about twenty pages thick. Most of it, I quickly discovered, was purely negative evidence. Daniel Wilson, one report revealed, hadn't voted in his home district since the time of his disappearance. Neither had he, according to the others, started any lawsuits, mortgaged any real estate, filed for bankruptcy, used his credit cards, joined the armed forces, opened any bank accounts, or taken out a marriage license. His driver's license had expired a year after he disappeared and had never been renewed. At the time of his disappearance he had no points on his license and no criminal record. Since then there had been no activity in his checking or savings accounts; the balances in each were under a hundred dollars. No income taxes or property taxes had been paid in seven years. In itself, none of this distinguished Daniel Wilson from somewhere between ten and fifteen percent of the population. I would need a lot more than this to convince a judge he was really dead.

Toward the bottom of the pile I found an interim report by "JBF," who I knew to be Jonathan Franklin, an investigator I could call. According to the report, at the time of his disappearance Wilson was thirty years old, short to medium height, wiry build, brown hair and eyes. Paper-clipped to the corner of the first page was a black-and-white wallet-size formal photo of Wilson in a suit and tie. From the date on the back it was probably his law school graduation portrait. Assuming he graduated at twenty-five, the picture was twelve years old. I had visions of carrying this little picture around the state, asking people if they'd ever seen this average-looking guy with glasses and brown hair before.

It was a pleasant-looking face; maybe a little bland, but very presentable. His cheeks were smooth and pink, and he looked closer to twenty, or even eighteen, than twenty-five. His glasses weren't the wire-rimmed ones that were fashionable when I was in college, or the high-tech rimless models the yuppies wore now, but good old-fashioned horn-rims. It was the kind of face clients would trust.

The family background was minimal. Wilson's father had died when he was a child; his mother was still living and worked cleaning offices in Center City. She lived in the Overbrook section of west Philadelphia. There was a sister, Lisa, two years older, a former nurse who now lived in a small town in the north-central part of the state. Neither Lisa nor Daniel had any children. Neither had ever been married.

Franklin had come up with some more about Wilson's grade and high school education. He was consistently a superior student; not brilliant, but always near the top of the class. He was seldom absent, hardly ever late with work assignments, and never a discipline problem. Several of his high school classmates had been contacted; they remembered him as serious and hardworking. He played no sports, but was active with the school literary magazine and the newspaper. He had a few dates, but no one remembered a steady girlfriend.

Except to tell me that he'd attended Gettysburg College, was secretary of the Photography Club, and obtained a degree in history, the college section was a blank. I wasn't surprised; in high school everybody knows everybody. But people are too busy in college to know more than a couple of people well. Investigating backgrounds at the college level is only helpful if the subject was very well known or if the school is very small. I was reading with only half my attention by then; the rest of my mind was trying to focus on what kind of man was behind that picture. What was the judge going to make of him? I hoped he wouldn't decide that Wilson was the kind of loner who would pull up stakes and disappear without a word to anybody.

The next section was hardly more help. After college, three years at Temple Law School, graduating about one-third of the way from the top. Passed the bar on the first try and set up practice in Center City with a classmate, Leo Strasnick. When Wilson disappeared five years later the partnership had three associates and had offices in Philadelphia and Norristown.

I rubbed my eyes and looked at my watch. It was nearly one, and this was my only business day before the day of the hearing. The rest of the file would have to wait.

My investigation got off on the right foot. Not only was Leo Strasnick available, he agreed to see me at four. His office was only a few blocks from the station.

I tried Shreiner's next.

"The Shreiner Security Agency. How may we help you?" a well-modulated female voice said. She sounded like a recording of herself.

"Mr. Franklin, please."

"And who may I say is calling?"

"Just say I'm calling regarding the Wilson case." I was curious to see if that would be enough to get me through.

"Yeah, this is Jon Franklin," was all he said, but it was enough. Something was bothering him. His words were unnaturally clipped and his voice was too loud and too fast.

"Hello, Jon, this is Dave Garrett—"

"You said you were calling about the Wilson matter."

"Yeah, right," I said as casually as I could. "Remember me, Jon? We worked together on those tools disappearing out of Sun Shipbuilding? I was—"

"I remember." Then his voice softened. "Dave, what do you have to do with this? We're not in the Wilson case."

"I've just taken it over." There was silence on the other end. "I've read your report and I assume there's more than is there." More silence. "Look, Jon, the case is coming up Monday, for Christ's sake. Cut me some slack."

"You want some advice? Don't take the case. It's more trouble than it's worth."

"The lawyer guaranteed payment," I said, being deliberately stupid.

"No amount of money is worth it." I'd been expecting him to say that, but coming from an experienced man at the biggest agency in the state, a fifteen-year veteran of the Philadelphia police, it was still unsettling.

"There's been a threat?"

"Nothing I'd talk about." I didn't know what he meant, but I was quick enough to realize that he wasn't going to explain himself.

"Can we get together somewhere?"

"I've told you all you need to know already," he said, and hung up.

I hoped he wasn't right.

2

FRIDAY, 1:00 P.M.

Suburban Station was dirty and the air was stale, but at least it was warm. By the time I'd walked half a block I was missing it.

Logically, I should have started at the end—seeing the scene, reviewing the evidence, and talking to the police. Once I decided if I was dealing with a murder, an accident, a suicide, or a disappearance, at least I would know what to look for. But there was only time enough to scramble around and look as fast as I could, hoping to turn up something. With a little luck, a pattern would emerge somewhere along the way.

Without any luck, I'd be on the witness stand Monday in my best suit, with a set, all-business expression on my face, and my dick in my hand. And my luck hadn't been good in the last couple of years.

Wilson's last known address was only about half a mile away. I caught a bus going up the Ben Franklin Parkway, got off just before the art museum, and walked to his old block.

Years ago, before the Depression, Wilson's old

neighborhood had been the southern boundary of the old Jewish area of north Philly. Then a few black families started moving in and the whites fled to the north, fighting a twenty-year delaying action as they retreated up Broad Street. No Russian general ever surrendered space for time as skillfully. Finally they succeeded in barricading themselves in the Northeast section by blocking any further northern expansion of the subway system. And now, as a final irony, their sons and daughters were moving back south again. After all, who wanted to be stuck way out in the Northeast with no subway?

The area surrounding the art museum had been attracting attention for several years, ever since Society Hill became a hundred percent gentrified. At the moment it was about one-tenth abandoned row houses and two-tenths expensive yuppie townhouse condos. The rest of the area was trying to make up its mind. A number of construction signs evidenced the hopes and greed of real estate brokers, banks, and contractors.

I turned onto his old block and tried to imagine how it must have looked when he lived there. It wasn't hard. Almost all of the houses were darkened with an undisturbed hundred-year layer of soot. Some windows were flanked by pale rectangular patches of brick where shutters had once been attached. Except for a pink-and-green corner grocery store, the block was mostly three-story brick row houses with small concrete porches. Every first floor and basement window had iron bars, and most of the doors had multiple locks. Some nice cars were parked on the street, the kinds that cost as much as houses used to, but they didn't look like they belonged there. The license plates announced dealerships in Chestnut Hill and King of Prussia; I assumed they belonged to yuppies who worked in offices on the Parkway and didn't want to spend fifteen dollars a day for garage parking. The cars that looked like they belonged there were old and tired, like the houses.

Wilson's old address was a converted row house with three apartments, separated from its neighbor to the east by a narrow alley. No one answered any of the buzzers. The side of the building was covered with graffiti to a height of six feet. Some car tires and a rusted bicycle frame protruded from the rest of the rubbish in the small backyard.

I looked around; no one was on the street. The time of year to do this sort of work was in the summer, when people are out. Every neighborhood has people who sit out on their porches and watch what goes on: housewives, retirees, the disabled. But none of them were crazy enough to be outside in twenty degrees with a brisk wind.

The light coating of snow crunched under my feet. I kept my head down, looking for patches of ice. The concrete sidewalk was in poor shape; too many tree roots and garbage, and not enough care.

I tried two houses before I could even get an answer, and three more where they'd never heard of Wilson. The cold was seeping around the buttons of my coat and cutting through my suit right to my skin. I decided to try a run-down three-story apartment building directly across the street, and then give up.

The front door opened into a small alcove. Beyond it was an oak door with carved trim, set with a big pane of glass with beveled edges. Through the glass I could see a dim hallway with red carpeting. There were five buzzers in the alcove; one had no name next to it and none of the other four answered. That's what you get, I told myself, for coming around in the middle of a weekday.

I was putting on my gloves again when I saw movement in the hallway. I tapped on the glass and a short black man, about fifty, opened the door. His remaining fringe of hair was gray, and an unlit cigar hung in the corner of his mouth. His right eye was covered by a black eye patch.

"Hi, my name is Dave Garrett. I'm looking for someone who used to live around here."

He pursed his lips and nodded thoughtfully; about what I couldn't imagine. But he held the door wider and motioned me inside.

"Thanks very much. It's a lot warmer in here."

"It's a cold one." His voice was soft and tired, like good blues late at night.

"The fellow I'm looking for lived across the street until seven years ago. You live around here then?"

"The wife and I moved in here when I came back from Korea, after I got outta the hospital." He said "Korea" with the emphasis on the first syllable.

"Fellow's name is Dan Wilson. A lawyer." I decided not to show the picture; it was so old and formal it wouldn't serve as much of a reminder. "Average height maybe a little on the short side, brown hair, clean-shaven, glasses, about thirty the last time he was seen."

"Now who you say you were?"

"I'm an investigator. His family hired me to try and find out what happened to him. He disappeared seven years ago and no one's heard from him since."

"Family hired you?"

"Yes, sir."

"I knew him. Met his momma, too. Said he was dead." I could hear suspicion.

"I know that's what she thinks," I said, lying just a little. "It may be true, for all I know." At least that was the truth. "But the thing is, there's a court hearing coming up. To declare him legally dead. So his money can be distributed to his heirs. And I'm supposed to find out what I can about what happened."

His voice was still soft, but it was less tired. "Well, now. I understand that. Yeah, I can talk to you 'bout him."

I got out a small notebook. I had a pocket tape recorder but I left it in my briefcase; it makes so many people freeze up. "That'd be great if you could give me a couple of minutes, Mr. . . ."

"Harrison. Gerald Harrison. Apartment one. Right here, first-floor front."

"Great. Now when did you meet him?"

"Oh, let's see. He lived there 'bout a year, year and a half, I guess. I seen him comin' and goin'. If he wasn't in a hurry we'd wind up talkin' for a few minutes, most nights. Helped me dig my car outta the snow once. I got a bad back; VA disability pension. Hurt in combat, you know. Right at the start of the war. At the Pusan perimeter." Again he emphasized the first syllable, but for all I knew, that was how to pronounce it. After all, he'd been there. "Seemed like a nice young fella. Even though he was a lawyer and all, he wasn't too busy for other folks, you know."

"Were you ever inside his place?"

"Not when he lived there. But after."

"Huh?"

"His momma come down and cleaned out his place right after he died. She said he was dead; killed by some gangsters. I saw her carrying stuff out and we started talkin'. She asked, could she hire me to help move the stuff? So I did. But I wouldn't take no money for it. She needed the help, and he was a nice boy."

"Tell me what was inside."

"She'd been working; a lot of stuff was already packed up in boxes. Like his personal stuff, you know. We loaded all that in her car. She said it was going to the Salvation Army. I packed up the furniture, books, the rest of his clothes, everything else."

"Where did it go?"

"She borrowed a little van from somebody. I didn't ask. I suppose it went to the Salvation Army, too. Except the books; the Public Library sent a truck around for them."

"What kind of books?"

"All kinds. College books. Law books. Lots of travel books. And picture books."

"What kind of pictures?"

"Books about picture taking. Photography. He was a real good picture taker. Took pictures of my grandchildren one time. Real nice pictures, too."

"Anything else you remember?"

"No. Well, he had a typewriter. Real fine one. Electric. His momma gave that to me."

"You still have it?"

"Yes, sir."

Just maybe this could be my lucky day. "Does it still have the ribbon that Wilson used?" I didn't have the resources myself, but the right lab could recreate everything that had been typed using that ribbon. It would take weeks, but with that kind of evidence it would be worth a continuance. I thought of what might be on it—a suicide note, a response to a demand for money, a farewell letter?

"No, sir. It was pretty faint. We got a new ribbon for it after a while. Threw the old one away. Did I do something wrong?"

Easy come, easy go. "No. There's no way you could have known not to do it. It's our fault for not coming around back then. Look, you said you saw him come and go?"

"Yes, sir."

"Tell me about his routine."

"Well, he drove to work. Kept his car parked right out front. There was lots more parking in those days. So anyway, I knowed when it was gone. He left for work early. Sometimes 'fore I got up. Come home late. I see him comin' home, seven, eight at night. He always wave to me if he see me. Worked a lot of Saturdays, too."

"Did he have many visitors?"

"No. Just the ladies."

"Tell me about them."

"Oh, there was several. A couple I only saw one time. But there was one blonde lady, with long hair, curly, you know. Named Elizabeth. I remember her because that's my granddaughter's name. Nice lady. He introduced me to her.''

''Do you remember her last name?''

''No. I'm sure sorry.''

''Anything else about her?''

''Just that she seemed nice. And she dressed well. They held hands a lot.''

''You said there were others?''

''A couple of them I only saw once or twice. But there was the other lady I saw once in a while. She came and went without him. Either she had a key or he left one for her with somebody.''

''Can you describe her?''

''I never saw her close up; only across the street. About his age. She had blond hair, but not as long as Elizabeth's. Real nice figure. Not too broad and not too narrow, if you know what I mean. And she knowed how to move it, too. Long legs, and she usually wore high heels. Fine lookin' woman. She wore good clothes, but not like the other lady. I mean, Elizabeth wore goin'-to-work clothes. This other lady wore, like, out-on-the-town clothes.''

''You mean, sexier clothes?''

''Yes, sir.'' His mouth was in a straight line now, and I saw that I'd pushed too hard. It was clear he wasn't going to discuss his observations about sexy-looking white women any further with a strange white man. I was momentarily startled; while we were talking I hadn't been conscious of his color. A white can forget the race of the person he's talking to. Blacks don't have that luxury.

''Did you get her name?''

''No. We was never introduced. I never spoke to her. She just came and went.''

"When his mother was there, did you ever meet his sister?"

"No, sir."

From what I knew of the file, it sounded like the woman might be Wilson's sister anyway. "And the other ladies?"

"Once or twice there were others. I didn't pay close attention," he insisted.

Like hell you didn't, I wanted to say, but kept it to myself. "Around the time he disappeared was there anything unusual around his place? Unusual visitors or noises late at night or anything like that?"

"No, sir. The blond lady I mentioned, besides Elizabeth, was around. But nothing else. No other visitors I seen."

Lisa was in town from LA then, so that might account for the unnamed blonde. "Did he have any male friends?"

"Once in a while somebody'd visit. A couple of times some men his age dropped him off. But not often. He never had no parties or anything like that."

"What did he do with his time?"

"When he wasn't working, I don't know. He was gone a lot. Travelin', he said."

"Where did he travel?"

"He didn't say. He said he was doin' a lot of traveling on weekends when he wasn't working. Like up to New York or upstate looking at them small towns."

"Did he go alone?"

"Far as I know. I never actually seen him leave

or get back. His car would be gone at funny times and then just be there again.''

''Funny times?''

''Like he'd leave and come back in the middle of the night; like take off Friday midnight and come back early Monday morning. Or leave real early Saturday morning and come back late Sunday night.''

''Any reason you can think of for that?''

''No, sir. 'Cept he was young and single. He had no ties.''

''Listen, you think of anything else, I'd appreciate it if you'd give me a call.'' I handed him a card. ''You can call anytime. If I'm not there you can leave a message on the answering machine.''

I thought of giving him ten dollars for his time, and then decided against it. He might be hurt and not able to chase women as well as he used to, but he had his pride. Instead, I spent ten minutes asking him about the Pusan perimeter.

I headed back toward the Parkway and stopped for a hot dog from a vendor. Even though it was well after noon, there was a line six deep waiting to be served. Everyone ahead of me was wearing an overcoat over a suit and tie. That's another funny thing about Philadelphia: It isn't a town that stops to eat during the day. If you want a two-hour business lunch, go to New York. You can walk around Center City on a nice day and see hundreds of business and professional people eating hot dogs and sausages and gulping down cans of soft drinks. Almost all of them are standing up, and most are walking somewhere while they eat. In the seventies, one of the local TV stations even had a regular show called "Sidewalk Gourmet," with tips on the best pushcarts. It boosted the station's ratings five percent all by itself.

Since I was on a case, I splurged—not only an Italian sausage, but coffee and a soft pretzel, too. With mustard, of course. By the time I finished my coffee the weather didn't seem so cold. I checked my watch; I still had some time left. What to do? I decided to play a long shot. The report from Shreiner's said that Wilson had banked at the First Pennsylvania Bank. There was a branch across the street, just visible on one of the little side streets, only a couple of blocks from Wilson's apartment. He might have banked over in Center City, near the courthouse and his office, but the local branch was worth a try.

When I stepped inside I decided it might not be such a long shot after all. It was a step back into the nineteenth century: heavy furniture, brass chandeliers, and dark wood paneling. Almost every lawyer has a sense of history; it's the nature of the profession. And unless he had some compelling reason to do his business in a glass-and-steel office building downtown, he likely would have come here. Two tellers were on duty; their combined ages probably didn't equal mine. There was no point in asking them what they were doing seven years ago—probably trying to grow breasts. But the customer service rep looked more promising—if age was the only criterion.

"Yes, may I help you, sir?" She was thin, stiff, and dry, with a voice to match. I wondered if she'd ever been as young as the kids in the teller cages. Even though I wasn't asked, I sat down. Her desk was one of those tiny models that banks issue their lower-level management people. They have no drawers and the employees get demerits if the top is untidy. It made me glad that I didn't work for a bank.

"Yes, my name is Garret. I'm an investigator engaged by the family of one of your depositors. He disappeared seven years ago."

If anything, she became even more dry. "Yes, sir."

"The man is Daniel Wilson. A lawyer. He lived not far from here. Our records indicate he used your bank, although I'm not sure if he used your branch."

She gave me the kind of look that most women reserve for small boys trying to look up their dresses. "You understand that information regarding depositors is confidential."

"I have all the information regarding his financial affairs already. The Shreiner Agency is very thorough." Both statements were true, taken separately.

She was impressed and relieved. "Oh, sir. The Shreiner Agency. Why, we have worked with them on many occasions. How may we help you today?"

"I'm looking for people who knew Mr. Wilson." I described him. This time I also brought out the photograph. She looked at it for a long time, as if she were thinking of buying it but didn't want to be overcharged.

"I knew the gentleman myself. Not too well, but I certainly remember him."

"Tell me what you can recall."

"First of all, you understand that I can't divulge

anything about his financial dealings. Even though you have it. I know it's silly, but we have our rules.''

''Of course. Now how did you know him?''

''This is a small branch, and I've held several positions here. When he first came in and opened his accounts, I was a teller. I remember him as being pleasant and friendly. And it was a bit unusual, at that time, to have an attorney living in the neighborhood.''

''His neighbors say he was a nice fellow.''

''Very nice. Never made others wait unnecessarily. Considerate of others. Always had his deposit slips made out before he got in line.''

Boy, I thought, this was the stuff of hard-hitting investigations. A few more leads like this and I could forget the case completely. ''Did he bank alone?''

''Oh, yes. Always.''

''Have you seen him in the last seven years?''

''No. And there's been no activity in the account—but of course you knew that.''

''You mentioned no activity in the account. Did you hear about what happened seven years ago?''

''It was in the papers that his car had been found and they thought he was dead. I remember reading it and thinking how sad it was, such a nice young man.''

''Do you recall seeing him around the time it happened?''

''Oh, yes. I remember it very well. It was the Friday before his car was found.''

''Anything special about that visit?'' I tried to sneak a look at my watch. Almost time to go.

"Just that he wanted to go to his safe-deposit box."

"The safe-deposit box?"

"Oh, yes. But I'm sure you knew about that already. Quite a large one. You know, most people just get those tiny ones, budget conscious, and then they run out of room and can't store all their important papers. But Mr. Wilson had the right idea; rented the largest size we have, right from the start."

"Oh, yes." I lied. "We knew there was a box, but not how large."

She indicated a series of four brass boxes on a sideboard against the wall. "The one on the right, there; about the size of four shoeboxes together; that's the size he had."

She was being conservative in her estimate; if you cut off Wilson's arms, legs, and head, you could probably hide his torso in the box. What did a young lawyer, single, living on the cheap, need with it?

"Did he use the box often?"

"Every time he made a deposit. He usually took about half his check in cash, and then went to his box."

"And he used it that Friday?"

"Yes, sir."

"Tell me what you remember about that visit."

"He came in just before the late afternoon rush. That was unusual in itself; he ordinarily banked just before we closed on Friday evenings. He cashed his entire check; no deposit, and asked to visit his box. He took two briefcases in with him. One was large, like a small suitcase—"

"A transfer case?"

"Yes, that's the word, thank you. He was in the room with his box a long time. When he left the cases seemed to be heavy."

"Did he say anything?"

"Just enough to do his business."

"Nothing about where he was going or why he was cleaning out his box?"

"Well, I don't know that he was," she said primly. "Speculation isn't a part of my job."

"Was he alone that time?"

"Oh, yes."

"Did he seem nervous or emotional?"

"Not that I can recall. He certainly wasn't unpleasant, if that's what you're asking."

I asked some more questions, but nothing that led anywhere. I thanked her and left.

I hit the street thinking that the case was starting to move; if I could just decide in what direction. I had no idea how he'd made his money, but enough cash to fill a briefcase and a transfer case was clearly enough to get out of town on. He didn't go anywhere in his car except to dump it, and he certainly wanted to get well away from his past life, so he must have taken some other form of transportation. I didn't think he'd steal a car from a friend—he was the kind of guy who would have felt obligated to return it. Besides, no such record of a friend missing a car had turned up in Shreiner's report. Using a rental car leaves a paper trail, and it always turns up somewhere. Trains and buses are too slow. Ships are mainly for couples on cruises; a single man traveling alone would stand out. That left airplanes as my best bet. I had friends at several ticket agencies with computers that could call up old data on tickets sold that weekend at the Philadelphia airport. If he'd used his own name, I could have a lead very soon. If that failed, I could check Newark, Baltimore, and New York.

My excitement was waning by the time I reached the end of the block. And what if he'd used a different name? Airlines don't ask for an ID if you pay cash, and he had plenty of cash. And even if I documented a one-way plane trip, it certainly wouldn't help my clients. The bank's evidence suggested a disappearance, not a death. Not that it made a difference, but it wasn't what I was being paid to look for. If that was the way it was, there was nothing I could do, but I hated the idea of charging someone to prove the other side's case. I consoled myself that at least I'd found something that Shreiner's hadn't.

I grabbed a bus and headed back for Center City.

The law firm of Wilson, Strasnick & Mendelson had half of the fifteenth floor of one of the new high rises near City Hall. Even by the standards of a Center City law office, it was imposing. Real Oriental rugs lay on top of the gray wall-to-wall carpeting, and the waiting room was done up as an Old English reading room, with dark paneling, brass wall sconces, and heavy, comfortable chairs and tables. On the wall across from me the magazine rack offered the current issues of *Forbes*, *Smithsonian*, *The New York Review of Books*, *Connoisseur*, and *Atlantic Monthly*. I felt out of place, even in my best suit. Fortunately, I was alone in the reception room.

A little after four, a blond receptionist who'd

stepped straight from the pages of a fashion magazine—with a side trip to the jewelers—ushered me into a conference room with a table big enough to seat twenty. It was simply furnished, but its sheer size, in downtown Philadelphia, spoke of even more money than the reception area. I became conscious of the stain on my tie.

A deeply tanned man in his middle thirties entered by another door and offered his hand. He wasn't wearing a suit jacket and he'd loosened his tie. He wore red suspenders. "Leo Strasnick, Mr. Garrett. Pleased to meet you."

The interesting thing was, he really was; or at least he seemed to be. His smile reached more than his mouth, or even his eyes; it gave a good-natured, wrinkled glow to his whole face. His dark hair, thinning a bit on the sides, was perfectly groomed. So were his nails, I noticed as my eye caught a gold pinky ring with a diamond. He looked strong and fit, and his shirt bulged at the top buttons. There was also some bulging at the bottom buttons. A few too many good meals at Le Bec Fin, I decided. I caught myself trying to pull in my own stomach.

We sat down at one corner of the table. "I appreciate your seeing me on short notice."

"We're really busy around here at this time of year. We're still digging out from all the year-end business we had. Actually, I'm in the middle of a settlement right now, but we're waiting for the title company to get a power of attorney up here, so I can give you a few minutes—at least till the documents arrive. I assume it's about Dan Wilson."

"There's a hearing scheduled for Monday. I'm trying to find out what happened."

"For the insurance company? I already gave them my statement."

"For the family."

"Yes, so you said." I gave him Mark Louchs's card. He glanced at it and handed it back.

"As I understand it, the life insurance is related to his partnership interest," I said.

"Oh, yes. It funds the buyout of his partnership share—gives the firm the money to finance a lump-sum settlement with him—or rather, his heirs. So if he is declared dead, the money goes to the firm and then to his estate."

"I assume the firm is the beneficiary, then?"

"I suppose. I would think so. Although we don't benefit; it's a pass-through situation. Now, then," he said more briskly. "What questions about Dan can I answer for you?"

"Let's start with how you met."

He glanced at his watch, just slowly enough to make sure I'd see it. "I'm not sure what that has to do with anything."

"The judges are hostile to these cases. Lots of people have been duly declared dead and then show up again. Very embarrassing for everyone, especially if insurance money has changed hands. So I need to know everything I can—any little thing that might help convince the judge he's really dead."

He nodded. "We met in first-year law school. Everybody was driven, of course, but he was even more so. Never let up. Not that he wasn't fun, you understand; always a good sense of humor, liked to joke, But just really serious. Even more than the married students with families to think about.''

''Whose idea was it to link up?''

''Mine.''

''Why?''

''I thought we'd make a good mix. He was sharp and a hard worker, but not a client getter. Too shy and standoffish. Clients think you're being aloof. I told him, I'll get them in the door, and we'll do the work together.''

''Any outside interests?''

''Not in law school that I knew of. All any of us did, back then, was work. But later, when we were in partnership, he loved to travel. Didn't matter where—driving around the area, trips to Europe, a week in Canada, anything to get out of town.''

''Did he do anything in particular on his trips? Make business contacts? Meet people? Bring back souvenirs?''

''Never mentioned anything but the usual travel stories: how the car broke down, how it rained in London, the food, things like that. He was never secretive about his trips. If you asked him on Monday where he'd been, he'd tell you. And if there was a good story, he'd tell the whole office.''

''Did he go alone?''

''As far as I knew. He never mentioned taking anyone.''

''Did he have girlfriends?''

''I don't recall if he dated in law school or not. But he had a decent social life as far as I could tell. There was one girl he dated for a year or so; we had them to the house once or twice.''

''Can you remember her name?''

"Sorry. It was a long time ago."

I tried not to think about how many times I'd be hearing that in the next three days. "Did he live alone?"

"That's one thing I know for certain. Never had a roommate. Of course, he really had no need."

"What do you mean?"

"Well, I mean no need in the sense that a lot of people need roommates to help with the rent. His expenses were low. He always lived very simply; drove an older car, lived in modest apartments. Never any real dumps, just efficiencies or small one-bedroom places."

"So what did he do with his money?"

"We didn't always do this well, Dave. The first five years were a struggle. Things have really only picked up in the last couple years. And we carry a lot of debt."

"What kind of work do you do?"

"General civil practice, with an emphasis on trial work. Personal injury, Jones Act, workmen's comp, commercial, construction cases, plus some office practice. Like the real estate settlement in the other conference room," he added pointedly.

"What about when he was with you?"

"The same. Just not as much of it, and the cases weren't as good."

"How was he as a lawyer?"

"Very good. Serious and careful. I miss having him around."

"What do you know about his disappearance?"

He looked down at the table again, but then raised his eyes. "I'll tell you what I can remember. My impression was that he was burning out. He was coming into the office late, which was unheard of for him, and stopped coming in on weekends at all. He seemed tired. He said he wasn't sleeping well. If I remember it right, he'd just broken up with the girl I mentioned. He asked to see a copy of the partnership agreement—said he wanted to review his options. It made me nervous, of course, but I gave it to him. Besides, I wasn't sure how serious he was about leaving. Certainly he didn't mention a definite decision or a date or anything like that. I would have sat down for a long talk with him if he'd said anything specific. I wanted him to stay. If he'd needed a couple months off to recharge his batteries, we could have worked it out. Anyway, he just disappeared. I'm sure you know about the business with the car. I don't know anything beyond what I've been told about that. I never heard from him again.''

"How close in time was this request for the partnership agreement to his disappearance?"

He thought for a moment. "The same week."

"Did you know his family?"

"He had a sister, I think. And his mother is still living. I don't recall ever meeting either of them."

"What's happened to his share of things since his disappearance?"

"According to our partnership agreement, the only entitlement to a share is upon death or withdrawal. There's nothing to administer for now."

"Can I have a copy?"

"Sorry, it's proprietary."

"Certainly. I understand." I knew he'd turn me down; perhaps now he'd give me what I really wanted. "Can you just tell me the amount of life insurance payable?"

"I believe it's one hundred thousand dollars."

"Did he have any enemies?"

"Oh, there were a couple of lawyers who bore grudges, and a disgruntled client or two, but no one ever made any threats that I was aware of. Certainly no one who would attempt to kill him."

"What do you think happened?"

He leaned back in his chair, away from me, and spread his hands palms upward. He shook his head. "What happened? I don't know. He was under a lot of pressure, working way too hard. I think he made some bad decisions."

"Meaning he staged this to cover his tracks and disappear?"

"No, nothing like that, I'm afraid."

"Then what?"

He looked me in the eye. "I think he committed suicide and tried to make it look like a murder."

"You'd better take this one step at a time."

"As far as suicide, well, he was very tense, very unhappy. He had no wife or children. No one to give him any perspective, take his mind off his troubles. These things sometimes happen. People blow small problems out of proportion. He was always a worrier. And as to why make it look like murder, or like an accident, I don't know. Maybe he thought suicide would be a shame to his family. He was very close to them. Many people still feel that way, you know. And besides, the insurance policy pays double for death by accident or homicide, and nothing in case of suicide except a refund of premiums." He paused, touching his fingertips together. ''I know that's not enough of a reason to kill yourself. And no, it doesn't make a lot of sense. But it makes more sense than any of the alternatives.''

He stood up and extended his hand. The fashion model was at the conference room door to show me out.

3

FRIDAY, 7:00 P.M.

I used a pay phone in the lobby to call the Powell Township Police Department. Although it was already after five, I had no trouble reaching the chief—he answered the phone himself. The officer who'd done the Wilson investigation was no longer around; he'd moved to Ohio a couple of years before. But the chief said he was familiar with the case and was working that night anyway. He agreed to meet me at seven.

The sun, a cold and burnt-orange ball, was hanging low to the west when I walked outside. Although it was an hour till sunset, the buildings had already darkened the street. Wind blew through my overcoat as I walked down JFK Boulevard toward my Honda. I'd found a space in an alley off Eighteenth Street behind a dumpster; when I got back, not only was the paint job still intact, but there was no ticket. It was enough to brighten my mood.

I headed west, out of the city. I lived in a down-at-heels garden apartment complex in an unfashionable part of the Main Line behind Radnor. My clothes, the furniture, and the Honda were all I had to show for my marriage. Well, not quite; it depends on whether you count my disbarment. My wife had wanted the Audi when we separated, even though we'd bought the Honda for her. It suited me; there was less money owing on the Honda. And it was a good car for my work. People will notice, sooner or later, if an Audi or BMW seems to be parked in one place very long. But a white Honda Civic with no window decals and no special antennas can sit for a week without anyone remembering it afterward.

Even though it was just after five, the traffic moved smoothly. Philadelphia's traffic is completely unpredictable. I used to think it was the unsynchronized traffic lights, but it's more than just that. There's a perversity about when the streets are busy and when they're not that defies the law of averages. You can be stuck in what looks like rush hour traffic on the Schuylkill or Roosevelt Avenue at seven in the morning, fight your way through to downtown, and find it deserted. And the next day it takes only ten minutes to get downtown, then half an hour in gridlock to get the last three blocks to your office.

I parked in the main parking lot in front of the complex. Even though I had an assigned space, I never parked there, or even where I'd parked the day before. When I was a lawyer, handling a tough domestic case for the wife, the husband looked up where I lived, slashed the Audi's tires, and pissed on the front seat. You learn from such things, especially if you drive the car afterward in hot weather.

The apartment wasn't dirty; neither was it clean.

Mainly it was dusty and unused. During the week I ate all my meals out, and I only cooked on weekends if there was no surveillance going on. Since that's what I did almost every Saturday night, the kitchen was hardly used. When I did eat at home, I usually ate off paper plates. I slept there, of course, except for the rare all-night stakeouts and the even rarer nights when a woman invited me home.

I got out of my suit and changed into jeans, insulated boots, a heavy flannel shirt, and a parka. I checked my answering machine and my answering service from the office; no messages of consequence.

Back at the car, I opened the trunk and made sure my equipment was still there. A 35mm camera with a zoom lens, flash attachment, and film—100 ASA black-and-white for daylight and detail work, infrared for night shots, and 400 ASA color, just in case. Two flashlights—a tiny pencil beam and an ordinary two-cell one when I felt like blending in. A box of long-play casette tapes and a pint bottle with a wide mouth for pissing in, both essential for stakeout work. A powerful set of night binoculars. Some people in the business recommended starlight scopes; my experience is that anyone you'll be watching at night is moving around in some sort of light anyway, usually streetlights or headlights, so a good pair of night binoculars is all you need. Plus, the scopes are expensive. The last item was an ordinary toolbox with a couple of wrenches, a socket set, a small hammer, some assorted screwdrivers, and the usual miscellany of picture hangers, screws, and washers. I never used any of the hardware; it was there only as camouflage for my burglar's tools. By themselves, the picks and pry-bars would have stood out. Not that I did many inside investigations, to use the euphemism, but every once in a while it went with the job.

I looked around the parking lot, satisfied myself that no one seemed to be watching, and started up. I liked to keep the inside of the car bare, as a precaution against theft and to keep the car from being noticed. All that was in the driver's compartment with me was an empty Thermos behind the passenger seat and a .357 magnum with a four-inch barrel under the driver's seat in a holster. I never carried the gun on a job, even though I had a license. For one thing, if you get yourself into a situation where you need a gun, you've made a mistake at the start. Second, Pennsylvania's laws on carrying a handgun are contradictory. A handgun license is statewide in scope; but it is also a misdemeanor to carry a gun within the city limits of Philadelphia—which is the place you need one the most anyway. No one has ever resolved the conflict, and I didn't feel like being the test case.

I made good time on the turnpike. By the time I reached the rest stop just before the Morgantown exit, I figured I had enough time for a hamburger. I ate with one hand and held open the police information part of the Shreiner file with the other.

It wasn't the actual report; under a peculiar Pennsylvania statute relating to police record-keeping, it would have been illegal for the police to allow that to be copied. But clearly the Shreiner people had seen the report, because their summary was pretty extensive.

A telephone call was received at Powell Township via county radio around 2230 hours mentioning an incident involving a car and a shooting on Route Ten near Mohnton Road. The caller, a female, gave her name as Lisa Wilson. Because it was a shooting, units from the state police and from the adjoining township, Brecknock, were also asked to respond. Sergeant Dietz arrived about ten minutes after the call was received. A Ford Pinto, four years old, was found in a patch of trees in a lane near the intersection. The driver's window and the passenger's window were both shattered, and there were two bullet holes in the front left fender above and to the rear of the wheel. The car was stuck in the mud but otherwise drivable. The keys were missing and the headlights were off. The transmission was in drive. Gas tank was half full. The front interior, especially the driver's side, was covered in blood. Because of "muddy conditions in the area and road traffic on Route Ten, it was impossible to identify any footprints or tire tracks as being associated with the vehicle."

I sighed and rubbed my eyes. I knew crap when I saw it. If the area was muddy, it would have held great footprints. Trouble is, if you step all over them with size twelve boots, all you get is size twelve footprints of yourself. I had met a hundred Sergeant Dietzes in my life; well-meaning but arrogant and ham-fisted. I was sure he roamed all over the scene with his piece out, playing hide-and-seek with his own shadow, until the state police arrived and called him a goddam dumb asshole for destroying evidence.

The rest was a summary of the lab reports. The

blood was human, type O positive, which narrowed the candidates down to about half the population of North America. The car was registered to Daniel Wilson. All of the identifiable prints in the car—which weren't many—were his. Examination of the engine compartment revealed two .45 bullets, both badly flattened by impact with the engine block. At least one of the rounds was a hollow-point, for enhanced expansion upon impact; the examiner wasn't sure about the other. End of file. Besides, it was time to be going.

I was surprised by the Powell Township Police Station. Most of the township police departments have a little office tacked onto the township sheds. This was a handsome, one-story building with polished brown linoleum floors and bright fluorescent lighting. The dispatcher on duty directed me to the chief.

His office was for work, not display. Wanted posters and missing children bulletins were thumbtacked, taped, or nailed to every vertical inch of wall space. Files, many of them capped with empty coffee cups, were piled everywhere; he had to clear a stack off one of the chairs so I could sit down. The air was thick with cigarette smoke, and I counted three overflowing ashtrays on his desk.

The chief—he introduced himself as Harry Ziemer—was a tall, beefy man, about fifty, his eyes in a permanent squint from too many years of traffic duty in the summer sun. He pumped my hand once, hard, and sat down. "Welcome to Powell Township, Mr. Garrett."

"I know this is short notice and that this is an

old file, Chief. Thanks for taking the time to meet with me.''

''Old, but still open.'' I saw the case folder sitting on the middle of his desk.

''I'd like to see it cleared as much as you would.''

''It's the only unsolved homicide in the township.'' It was a simple statement of fact, but it sounded like a response to an accusation. I wondered if the township supervisors or the DA was riding him about the case, or if this was purely a matter of professional pride.

''So you think it was a homicide?''

He didn't respond right away, and when he spoke, it was slowly. He watched me while he talked. ''Well, I start out thinkin' that way.''

I looked at him and then at the file, wondering what was inside. ''This thing cause much of a fuss when it happened?''

''Oh, yeah; not the shooting itself—victim wasn't from around here, you know. But the not finding the body, now. Gets all the speculation going. And the big-city TV reporters out here for their story, too.'' His voice had the pleasant, singsong rhythm of the Pennsylvania Dutch, but his tone wasn't pleasant. ''Lots of stupid-ass questions, most of them by fellers I thought were pretty smart. Trying to make this place look like a dumping ground for Philadelphia killings.''

''Chief, I'm not out to give anybody any publicity about anything. I work for the survivors of this fellow, trying to help them. His mother and sister. This hearing I told you about on the phone—well, if the judge thinks that Wilson is really dead, then he'll release the life insurance money and anything else that's been tied up all these years. Help out the living. I'd just like you to tell me what you've got. Maybe it'll help me, maybe not."

"My department's looked bad enough out of this. And I wasn't even chief back then."

"If I can help clear this case there'll be lots of good publicity. And you're the chief now." It sounded too blatant, so I decided to back off. "But the main thing," I added, "the main thing is that it really can't hurt the township; it can only help. And no one has to testify. I just need to know what you know."

"What I tell you is off the record?"

I nodded. He paused for a moment, and then nodded back. He put on his reading glasses and opened the file. I told him what I knew already. He nodded slowly as I spoke, thumbing through the pages. When I finished he put aside most of the file and left a few sheets and a big envelope between us.

"Here's what else we got. The stateys went over the car real careful, now. There was a fourth bullet. It nicked the left post of the windshield at about eye level. Like the others, it was moving perpendicular to the car, left to right. After the nick it kept on going; no bullet recovered. But the lead tracing matched the slugs from the engine. One shell casing was found at the scene, a forty-five. No reloadings. They found hair samples from at least two different people in the car. But that don't mean shit; anybody that gets in your car can leave a hair or two, and they can stay there for months. For what it's worth, one sample was short, dark, and brown; another was long and blond. We matched up the blond sample by microscopic comparison with a former girlfriend, Elizabeth Chatwin; the other was the victim's. There was no firing inside the car. There were very faint powder markings on the left side of the car and on the outside of the glass fragments from the driver's window. Not concentrated around the bullet strikes; more spread out. It's not in the report, and the criminologist said she wouldn't say this in a criminal case, but she thinks it means that the vehicle was moving when the bullets struck. The shots were from fairly close range to leave any powder residue, but without knowing the wind speed and whether the shots came from a moving vehicle, she won't even try to guess on the range. No more than five feet, though.''

''What about powder marks on the driver's window?''

He laughed. ''Oh, yeah, Dietz was interested in that, too. The fragments from the driver's door went inward; they were mainly inside the car. The ones from the passenger's side went outward, all over the road. He got together all the glass fragments—some off the road and some from the inside of the car—and shipped them off to the FBI crime lab in Washington in two envelopes. Asked them to please reconstruct the window and test it for powder and the angle of the bullet. The package came right back, along with a note telling us we had to be kidding. When I opened it I saw what they meant. Your car windshield is safety glass; it's got a layer of plasticlike stuff in between two layers of glass. So it stays together even when it breaks. But your side windows are tempered glass; they shatter into a million little pieces. No way you'll ever piece them together. All we can tell is, a bullet or some other object came in the driver's window, went through the occupant, and out the other side.''

He put the report to one side and passed me the photographs. I had seen dozens of these in the past, state police black-and-white eight-by-ten glossies and yet being handed a packet of them always made my stomach jump. You could look at two or three perfectly ordinary shots of a damaged car, just like you would see in the morning paper, and the next one would be a decapitated corpse. Or a skeleton trying to get out of a burned-out pickup truck, its bony hand on the door handle that a few hours before had been too hot for him to touch. Or just a photograph of a shoe lying in the road, a long way from the impact, with a foot in it.

These were bloody, of course, but nothing like what I'd seen before. The first one showed the Pinto from the side, most of the detail washed out. The illumination seemed to be from the headlights of a patrol car. Yet the two bullet holes in the fender showed up clearly, round and black as a pair of eyes. The car was nose-down and tilted slightly to the right, I assumed because the ground was lower where the right side wheels were.

The next few shots were close-ups of the fender holes, some from the outside and some taken with the hood open. In several, someone had passed string through the holes to the points where the rounds struck the engine, indicating the paths the bullets had taken. I was surprised; normally they go to this kind of trouble only to document the path of rounds through a human body. The strings indicated that the rounds had come from slightly to the rear. The next shot showed the strings as seen from the front of the car, looking back at their level. The strings were pointing up at a noticeable angle, maybe thirty degrees, indicating that the bullets had been fired from above. Then I realized the car was tilted, too; if it was level the strings would be only slightly tilted. So the shooter was a little above the level of where the bullets hit. If the car was level when they were fired, that is. You could get a headache thinking about reconstruction too much. The main thing was that the strings nearly met at a point a few feet away from the car, indicating that all of the rounds had been fired from approximately the same place relative to the Pinto. That meant the shooter was moving at roughly the same speed as the Pinto, and that the shooter squeezed off all four rounds very quickly.

There were several interior shots of the car; the lighting was very good, probably with some kind of bounce flash. Blood was splattered and smeared everywhere around the front seat. There was not much else to see. I handed them back.

"Any neutral witness statements?"

"No. The area is rural. Nearest house is a half mile away, and it's mostly forested. Blankets the noise. People might not have heard anything at a quarter of a mile. We talked to the nearest residents anyway; nobody could add a thing."

"What about Lisa Wilson's statement?"

His eyebrows knitted. "Isn't she your client?"

"Yes and no. I represent the heirs. If the victim left no will it all goes to his mom. If he left a will then the sister might stand to benefit, if he put her in. I don't know. But anyway, I haven't talked to her yet. Not till tomorrow morning. I'd like to know what she said that evening.''

The chief nodded. Like most policemen—or lawyers, for that matter—he had great faith in the first version witnesses tell, no matter how fragmentary or confused, before they have time to think about what story would suit their interests best. He picked up a two-page typewritten report with a signature at the bottom.

''I'm not going to read all the crap. The investigating officer wasted a lot of time here. Even gave her the Miranda warnings. Anyway, here we go. Statement was taken at the station here starting at about twenty-three-thirty hours. Witness had arrived at the station at twenty-three-hundred hours and had to wait for Dietz to return from the scene of the investigation. Witness says she had been shopping. She was in Philadelphia for a visit. The victim and the witness were in separate cars. He had his own car, the Pinto; she was driving a Chevy registered to her mother. Witness produced her mother's registration for the Chevy. Were supposed to meet in Morgantown and she was to follow him to a restaurant. He didn't show up; she waited and waited. Tried to call his office, his home, her mother, trying to find where he was. She drove around Morgantown looking for his car. Finally she started up the nearest main road, being Route Ten, northbound, thinking she may have misunderstood. Found car, no one around, no body. Had seen a couple of sets of southbound headlights go past her as she approached scene but thought nothing of it.

Then she called nine-one-one, who put her in touch with our township. She drove in to the station on her own after making her call. Very upset. Said victim had been in good spirits, didn't see very often since her move, had no reason to think he was in danger. No leads re enemies. Victim was lawyer in Philadelphia; unsure if handled drug or organized crime cases. There's more, about his address and stuff like that.'' He put the report back in the file and shut it with finality.

"Mr. Garrett, a couple of things I didn't mention. We didn't put them in the report because they might have given a defense lawyer ammunition if we ever charged anybody. Dietz was suspicious of her. Not for any particular reason; she seemed like a really nice girl, and really upset. She wasn't a real suspect, but she was all we had. He checked the backseat of her car. With her consent, of course. It was full of shopping bags. Dated receipts showing she'd been shopping that day. Women's clothes, mostly. Some of the receipts have the time as well as the date, you know. She'd shopped in the Reading outlet malls in the morning and at Park City over in Lancaster in the afternoon. And we checked her for powder; just a real basic rub-down test. The test gives a lot of false positives, but not this one. Negative. She hadn't fired a gun or been near anyone firing a gun.''

"You didn't let anything pass."

"With no witnesses, a car that looks like its been shot from close range? What would you think?''

"Are there any restaurants in the area?''

"Yeah. Three nice ones, Gentry, White Bear,

and the Country Chef. Fancy places with French food stuff.''

"Would they have been easy to find?"

"No, not really. All on back roads in the country. Lots of turns and forks.''

"Too bad it's been so long. About the restaurant story, I mean.''

He smiled. "Ah, we ain't so dumb, now. We checked; there was a reservation for two at the Country Chef for eight o'clock for Wilson. No one showed up. Hostess remembered it 'cause they were so busy that night that they held the table for ten minutes and then gave it to somebody else. They were afraid he'd show up a little late and be mad, but he never did. Reservation had been made several days before. She didn't remember real clear, but thought it was a man. Didn't give a first name, but the hostess remembered he was polite and well-spoken. And that the connection wasn't the greatest, like he might be calling from Philly.''

It was getting late, and I could see that the chief had given me all he had. "One more question, Chief. Well, two if you count directions. What do you think?''

He shrugged his shoulders. "There was talk, rumors, that it might be organized crime. You hear talk all the time. Especially about doings over there.'' He jerked his head in the direction of Reading. "But we could never pin anything down. Mainly, it didn't look like a mob killing. They either leave the body at the scene or kidnap the victim, kill him elsewhere, and hide the body. Pretty half-baked stuff, this, if it was organized crime. So there was no obvious motive and the MO was wrong.''

"The sister?''

He shook his head decisively. "Didn't see her that night, but I met her later on a reinterview a week or so later, when Dietz was unavailable. She wouldn't hurt a fly. Really sweet girl. Wish my own daughter was half that nice. Plus, if she had done it, she was smart enough to come up with a better story.''

"So then what?''

"Random killing. Some crazy man, driving by, not from around here, picks out Mr. Wilson. Drives past, or hides by the side of the road, pulls out a forty-five. Could have been back in New Jersey or Maryland within an hour.'' He said it as if being from New Jersey or Maryland was in itself sufficient motivation for being a random killer.

"What about the body?''

"This is pretty rough country. Not so good for farming, not like down in Lancaster. Could have put it in an old well or a mine shaft. Used to be mining around here, but no more. Or dumped it in a quarry—couple of abandoned ones around here, flooded up. Even might stick it in a ravine if he didn't mind the chance that some hunter would find it. Or took it with him. Who can say about crazy people?''

"There's no telling what crazy people will do.'' Or sane ones, for that matter, if they're pressed hard enough. It seemed as good as Strasnick's theory. Or any I had, for that matter. I took directions, thanked him, and headed out.

It was fortunate that Route Ten ran beside the

station, and that all I had to do was follow it. In the next seven miles I saw less than a dozen signs of human habitation, and no streetlights or signs at all. The only other traffic was a single set of headlights behind me. The road rose, fell, and twisted as if it were trying to throw me. Once I failed to appreciate how quickly a turn was coming up, braked hard, and skidded right up to a stone wall. From the paint smears on the stone, it appeared that others hadn't been so lucky. Large trees, mostly pines, lined both sides of the road and seemed to meet overhead.

He had said I'd be in Morgantown a half mile beyond the spot if I missed it, and sure enough— the road curved to the left one last time, straightened, and brought me right up to the turnpike tollbooths. I turned around, watched my odometer carefully, and found it on the second try. I drove by it slowly a couple of times each way and then got out.

Even by Route Ten standards, it was a desolate place. It was not even a true intersection; the other road was simply a muddy path, graveled in spots, heading generally toward the east. Coming from the south, the main road was in the middle of a long left-hand curve where it intersected the path. Looking further north, the road went over a crest and out of sight about a hundred yards away. Heavy pines on both sides. To the east of the curve the land was flat, but to the west across the road, it sloped upward to a bank about twenty feet high. About half the area was covered with a thin coat of snow; the rest was either bare or ice puddles.

The intersection itself was broad and flat enough

for several cars to park; it must be a popular place during deer season, I thought. I stood about where I figured the Pinto had been; big trees to the north and south obscured the view from both directions. It was easy to see it as you passed by, but not on either approach.

I opened my trunk and took out a hundred-yard steel tape and my big flashlight. I was about to turn on the light when the three-quarter moon came out between two clouds. The additional light wasn't much, but it was enough for something shiny to catch my peripheral vision—where night vision is best anyway. Without turning my head, I looked to my left.

Up on the bank, about thirty to forty yards from me, was the top of a car; not the grill or hood, just the windshield. It was facing directly toward me, but parked back from the edge of the bank. No lights.

No cars had passed me in either direction since I'd stopped. A car had been behind me when I left the police station. I struggled to recall; no, it hadn't been behind me when I turned around at Morgantown. There was no good reason for that car to be up there, if it was the same one. Well, not exactly; maybe a couple of teenagers looking for a place to park happened to follow me. And maybe not.

I reached into the trunk once more, pulled out a piece of twine and a small grease pencil, replaced the big light with my pencil light, and slammed the lid as hard as I could. The sound echoed for a moment, bouncing back once before being absorbed by the trees. I thought about how the four shots that night must have sounded. Then, as casually as

I could, I opened the driver's door and leaned in. Keeping my body between the seat and the other car, I reached quickly under the seat and scooped up my .357 magnum. On the off chance they had a starlite scope or some kind of infrared, I jammed it into a pocket of the parka before turning around.

Turning on the flashlight, I measured the distance between the road and the closest tree, then the width of the path where the trees ended. I held up a little notebook and a pencil but didn't bother to write anything down. There was no activity from the car. I walked down the path about ten yards, moving the flashlight from side to side. Stepping behind a tree, I looked back; the car was barely visible through the network of branches. I found a small rock for a weight and tied it and the flashlight to the end of a branch. It hung down to waist level and swung convincingly back and forth in the light breeze. I looked at my watch; I figured I had ten minutes, maybe fifteen, before they would become suspicious.

My first instinct was to drop to my hands and knees, or at least a crouch, but that might have made me visible underneath the canopy of pine branches. So I just moved slowly from tree to tree, avoiding the middle of the path, until I was another twenty yards down the trail. Just ahead, I could see where it ended in a clearing full of wrecked cars and rusted washing machines. Someone's dream of a cabin in the woods that never came off.

When I was sure I was out of sight, I headed north through the trees, moving as quickly as I could in the dark. Fortunately the ground was flat, and moonlight reflected off the dusting of snow. I didn't care how much noise I made as long as I couldn't be seen. When I estimated I'd gone about fifty yards, I cut to the left. Moving more and more carefully as I approached the road, I dropped to my knees and then to my belly. The car wasn't visible; unless it had moved, it was out of sight to my left around the curve of the bank. I crawled out to the very edge of the road. Still nothing. Moving as slowly as I dared, I inched out onto the road. I felt safer; the pavement was warmer than the snow, and would provide less contrast for an infrared scanner. Plus, my parka would blend into the black pavement.

The bank was steep, but thick with grasses, weeds, and branches; it was easy to climb. I reached the top, waited for the moon to pass into another cloud, and stuck my head slowly up over the rim.

At some point, years ago, the area had been bull-dozed and cleared—probably for houses. It was flat as far as I could see, at least a hundred yards, and there was a view of Morgantown and a valley. I could even see a glimpse of the turnpike. I looked away quickly to preserve my night vision. The car was about thirty yards away, directly across the road from my car, facing east. The engine was running, but no lights were on. No one appeared to be outside.

I pulled out the gun and eased myself up off the bank and onto the flat. Lying prone, I counted off sixty seconds. The snow began to seep through the cuffs in my parka and the gaps between the buttons. There was no movement from the car. Very slowly, I got up into a low crouch and circled around to the rear. If they were watching for me on the path, they would likely be paying no attention behind. If it was a couple of kids, it didn't matter anyway.

I worked my way around to the rear of the car, keeping about thirty yards away, checking around for backup; there was none. I avoided staying directly behind the car. There was always the chance that the moon would come out at the moment the driver decided to check his rearview mirror. Instead, I got down on my stomach and crawled up until I was nearly at the right rear wheel. Again, I counted to sixty. I kept the gun trained on the passenger's door at waist level.

I checked the moon; it was behind a large cloud. No danger of an inopportune appearance. Very slowly I got on one knee and looked into the car. I kept the gun at knee level; no point in presenting any metal surfaces to catch light.

The instrument lights were on. Two large figures, presumably men, were in the front seat. The driver was wearing a hat. The passenger was looking down in the direction of my car with some kind of viewing scope. There was no way to tell what it was except that some kind of power cord ran from it to the dash. The driver was holding a telephone to his ear. I looked at the roof: cellular phone and CB antennas, plus a third antenna I didn't recognize.

I got back down and away a few yards. The car was a new Ford Taurus, four-door, either white or beige. The license plate frame was from a Philadelphia dealership. Using the grease pencil, I took down the number on my forearm. Then I carefully backed away and retraced my path across the road.

I waited again for a minute before approaching my flashlight. When I was satisfied I was still alone, I put my gun back in my parka, retrieved the flashlight, and went back to my car.

I would have felt better checking the engine for signs of a bomb, but there was no way to do that inconspicuously; it was little comfort to think that if they wanted me dead they could have picked me off from across the road. The engine started fine, and I thought about my next move. Driving back to the police station would bring them along; but then what? The chief would have them stopped and get their IDs. They would turn out to be two clean-cut young fellows from South Philadelphia in suits and ties, who would claim they were checking out prospects for real estate development. And the hell of it was, in addition to shadowing me, it might very well be true. Any firearms in the car would be registered and licensed. The bills of sale were probably in the trunk.

There was nothing to be done. I turned left and headed south to the turnpike; keeping a careful distance, they followed. At the Valley Forge exit I lost them by running the tollbooth. I didn't expect to sleep much that night, but I went home anyway. There was nowhere else to go.

4

SATURDAY, 7:00 A.M.

I awoke at three, tried to get back to sleep till four, and gave up. I was restless, jumpy, and more than a little scared. I was being watched and I didn't know why. The fact that they were doing nothing more than watching was no consolation; if they were who I thought they were, there would be no warning if they decided to take me out. I had one foot in the grave already. I wished I knew the reason.

I took a long shower. If the organization was watching me, they wanted something. Information. It had to be about the Wilson case; I'd never been involved in any other case that could possibly interest them. I could tell them nothing because I didn't know anything—but maybe their watching me told me something. It made hash of the chief's random killer theory, at any rate.

I put on a pot of coffee and shaved, looking at my reflection as if it would help answer my questions. Was the chief's theory really so impossible? Suppose the organization was interested in Wilson, not necessarily with murder in mind, and then he happened to get killed by a random third party? With no body, they'd never believe it; they'd assume it was staged to cover his disappearance. Could be, but the odds were just too great. I had to eliminate some possibilities. There was so little time. But what if there were two competing organizations; group A got him; group B was now trying to find out what happened. Okay, so who was trailing me? People trying to get information or people trying to keep me from getting any? And what about the disappearing money? Had he suspected someone was after him? The police records had no mention anywhere of finding the cash or the briefcases. Could someone have known about them? Was it murder with robbery as a motive? Then why hide the body? Maybe someone knew he had the money, but when they stopped him, it wasn't on him. They might have worked him over at the scene or shot him in the course of stopping him. That would explain the blood in the car. And if he wouldn't talk, they took him somewhere to squeeze the location out of him. So no body.

I scrambled a four-egg omelet and put on some bacon. When I'd been married I worried a lot about cholesterol; I didn't care much anymore.

Were the people in the car from the same group that warned off the Shreiner Agency, or a different group? I wasn't sure which was more dangerous from my point of view. The group trying to obstruct things might leave me be unless I got close to something big; the others might put the squeeze on me regardless. And after they had what I knew—or rather, when they found out I really knew nothing—my life expectancy could be very short.

I put the food down in front of the window and ate. It was about five-thirty and the sky was beginning to lighten. I had a bad feeling about this case already. Before it was over, maybe even before this day was over, there would be trouble; but for now the coffee was hot and the eggs tasted good. I ate slowly, taking in the early-morning light and the silence of the streets.

I thought about walking away from it, of course. If it was a matter of my personal safety, I didn't care all that much about Dan Wilson and whether he would get away with it—if he *was* getting away. I was no hero. I even reached for Louchs's card once; then I thought through what kind of conversation it would be. Mark, I'm getting out. Oh, quitting on me at the last moment, huh? No, it's just that it's getting too dangerous. So that makes you as gutless as the Shreiner Agency and stupid, too; you knew what you were getting into at the start.

I knew Louchs wouldn't say anything like that, of course, but he'd be thinking it, and so would I. It reminded me of my days, long ago, with the Marines. My squad searched tunnels, rushed tree lines, called in artillery nearly on top of ourselves, jumped feet first into bunkers—and none of us thought of ourselves as brave. We did it because we were afraid to let the others know how scared we were.

Maybe it was a random killing after all, and the boys in the car were interested in me for some other reason. I shook my head; I was back where I started. Or was there a killing at all? The actual evidence that a death had occurred was minimal. Anyone serious about disappearing, especially fearing the mob was after him, could go to the trouble of staging what the police had found. The money angle fit. Wilson hadn't gone to the bank on a lark. He'd been there with good reason, and he hadn't intended to come back. But even the bank proved nothing. Maybe he was trying to disappear when whoever he was running from caught up with him.

Although I'd never had any dealings directly with organized crime, I had a contact. He was expensive, but sometimes for the right price he could come up with good inside information. He knew nothing himself; he was more of an information broker. A call to him meant a wait of hours or even days while he checked his own sources. I decided to call him later that morning.

I dressed in corduroy slacks, a tweed jacket, and a tie. The subject's sister was a nurse, used to dealing with professionals, and she would expect a tie. As I put on my jacket, I thought about carrying my second gun, a .380 automatic. I decided against it; if the pros wanted me dead I'd never see it coming anyway. They didn't get to be pros by shooting it out face-to-face at thirty paces on the main street at high noon. An ice pick in the back of the head, preferably when the victim was already unconscious or tied up, was more their style. I put on my overcoat and headed into the weather. When I stopped outside I was glad I'd taken my heavy coat.

I popped the hood and checked; no tampering that I could see. As additional insurance, I tore a thin strip of paper out of a road map and placed it so that it was caught between the hood and the body when the hood was down. If it disappeared I'd know the hood had been opened.

I wasn't proud of my office building, but there was no other place to meet. I was one of five tenants in an old house in west Philly; we shared an inadequate parking lot and a receptionist/secretary who was worse. It was the kind of place where you had to keep an eye on your hat and coat even in your own office. The other tenants were a decertified CPA who worked as a tax preparer, a passport photograph operation, a real estate broker specializing in apartment rentals to deadbeats, and a "credit counseling" agency. The last two shared most of the same clientele, or at least it seemed that way. The fifth tenant always paid his rent and assessments on time, but was never there. I once asked him his business; he smiled and said something about venture capital. I didn't ask again.

I was nearly half an hour early; I'd wanted a few minutes to collect my thoughts and review the Shreiner file again. But as soon as I locked my car door I heard another car door close right behind mine.

I turned and saw a woman in a red down jacket, jeans, and hiking boots. "Hi, you must be Mr. Garrett. I'm Lisa Wilson."

It was a low, pleasant, no-nonsense voice, a little nervous. I looked into dark brown eyes, framed by thick chestnut hair that reached below her shoulders. A thin, serious face with high cheekbones. Her mouth was set in a tentative smile and her hand was extended; I shook it. "Nice to meet you, Miss Wilson."

I unlocked the three bolts that kept the main en-

trance reasonably secure and motioned her inside.
"Go to the top of the stairs and I'll be right with
you."

She hung her jacket on the coatrack just inside
the door—it would be safe enough on a Saturday
with the building locked—and headed up the stairs.
She was wearing a clinging white turtleneck, and I
stopped to admire the view. She had high, full
breasts, a narrow waist, and narrow hips. There
was a rawboned, athletic, outdoors look about her
that I liked. She took the stairs ahead of me with a
loose, bouncy stride, two at a time while I watched
from behind. I'd never laid a hand on a client, either
as an attorney or as a private investigator, and I
wasn't going to start now; but she certainly helped
my spirits. Watching her was a hell of a lot more
interesting than crawling around in the snow trying
to keep one step ahead of the men in the car.

I unlocked the door to my office and ushered her
inside. Even though she was casually dressed, I was
never more aware of the shabbiness of where I did
my business: worn carpeting, a scarred desk, and
a water-stained ceiling. I hung up my own coat behind the door—I never left my own downstairs,
from force of habit—took out a yellow legal pad,
and sat behind the desk.

"Thanks for coming down so early."

"Thank you for taking such an interest in my
brother's case."

"We only have a short time."

"Yes, I know. But I don't think that the other
agency would have gotten up this early."

I smiled. "All right, then. Now you're aware of
the nature of what I'm going to be asking about?"

She stopped smiling, but her voice didn't waver. "You want to know what I know about Danny's death."

"Do you think he's dead?"

"Oh, yes. I mean, how could he not be? Don't you?"

"I don't have an opinion yet. And even if I did, what I think doesn't matter. We need to convince a judge. And they're very skeptical about cases like this. What we really have is just a disappearance, plus an absence of seven years. There's no real proof of death."

She crossed her legs and wound her fingers together around one knee. She looked away from me and her voice dropped. "Mr. Garrett, there's something I need to ask before we go any further."

I knew what was probably coming. Thanks a lot, Mark. "Sure."

"Our attorney said that you were very good." I waited for the rest. "He also said that you had been a lawyer yourself."

I measured my words carefully. "As far as how good I am, I'll leave that to your judgment. And yes, I used to practice."

She blushed and looked down at her hands. "I'm really sorry; I hardly know you. But if I'm going to—could you please tell me why you're not a lawyer anymore? This is really out of line, but Mr. Louchs said the Shreiner Agency would be so good, and they dumped us at the last minute. Then he called me and told me he'd just hired you. He said that you were really on the ball—that you used to be an attorney. So I asked him. He said I should ask you if I wanted to know. I hope you're not offended.''

"I was disbarred for dishonesty.'' The room was very quiet. I could hear the morning traffic picking up outside. She was still looking at her hands.

"I got out of law school fifteen years ago. I got married right after graduation; my wife was a social worker then. After we'd been married a few years she decided to try law school. When she finished, she took the bar and failed. Six months later she failed again, and the next time. She flunked it seven times in all. She was very bright; it was a test anxiety problem. And it got worse with each attempt. She wouldn't sleep for days, couldn't hold anything down, had anxiety attacks. She was seeing a psychiatrist. After the seventh failure she had to be hospitalized for a few days. Too many sleeping pills. Not really enough to kill her, but they were concerned. Mostly the hospitalization, after they treated the overdose, was for her depression. When she got out she asked me to take it for her; I said no. It was months before the next test date came around; by the time it did I said I would. You should have seen how happy she was. I passed it for her, but they were keeping an eye on repeaters. They caught us and disbarred both of us.''

"Oh.''

"I exhausted my appeals and had to turn in my license, withdraw from my firm. She left. Couldn't stand the guilt.''

"I'm sorry. I didn't mean to—''

"It's okay. It was my decision and I knew the risks.''

"You're a very strong person, Mr. Garrett.''

"No. I just know what I can change and what I can't."

"Okay," she said. "Let's go on then."

I picked up my pencil. "Were you and your brother close?"

"Oh, yes. As close as you can be living across country, at least. I came home once a year and spent time with him and Mom."

"When did you move away?"

She squinted at nothing, trying to remember. "I did two years of community college here, then I moved to Los Angeles for an R.N. program. That would have been, let's see, nineteen years ago this September."

"And you came home for the holidays each year?"

"Yes. I'd stay with my mom, visit old friends, see my brother, things like that."

"Did you write or call him regularly during the year?"

"On our birthdays or if there was a special occasion; not otherwise."

"The last vacation you were together, how did he seem?"

"He was never really a happy person, Mr. Garrett. He liked his work, and he didn't mope around, but he never exactly bubbled over. The last time, he was the same as always."

"What was he depressed about?"

Her look contained a hint of impatience. "People don't decide to get depressed any more than they decide to get happy. You just are a certain way. Growing up was really hard for both of us, but especially him. Our dad died when he was six. Even before he died, he'd stopped being much of a father to us. He was too sick and too wrapped up in his own problems to care about us. I had Mom; Dan didn't really have anyone. Mom had to work two jobs, and even as a little kid I was busy helping run the house; there was no time for anything back then.''

''All that's pretty old stuff.''

''There's things you can decide to change about yourself and things you can't. Dan was a quiet child, keeping to himself, and he never changed. By the time he was grown up, when he disappeared, most of his friends were married, with children. He hadn't found anyone. He just didn't feel he fit in.''

''Do you think he could have faked his death and disappeared?''

''I really don't know. But I don't think so. He would have told me if he had been thinking about it.''

''Okay, then, tell me what happened.''

''Like I told the Shreiner man, I had been shopping, first at the outlets in Reading and then over near Lancaster at the big mall. Things are so much cheaper here than in Los Angeles. We had agreed to go to dinner; he said he knew a great country restaurant. It was hard to find, so we were supposed to meet where Route Ten and the turnpike meet near Morgantown. He was going to lead me. I waited for an hour, hour and a half. I wasn't worried at first; he was very busy and something could have delayed him at work, even on a Saturday. It had happened before, many times, over the years. He was really conscientious about his clients and about getting his work done. I sat in the car and read a paperback book. But after a while, I started to be concerned. I called everywhere looking for him. It took half a dozen calls to confirm that no one had seen him. I knew the restaurant was somewhere north on Ten, so after some driving around I headed up that way. I figured I could always get directions at a gas station or somewhere. That's when I found the car. Bullet holes and blood but nothing else.''

"What did you do?''

"I got out and looked around for a while. Then I drove back to Morgantown and called the police. After that I called my mom, then went to the police station and gave my statement. I can't remember the name of the police department, but I'm sure you have that somewhere.''

"See any footprints or drag marks or anything like that?''

"I'm a nurse, Mr. Garrett, not a detective. I was scared and cold and not paying much attention.'' She softened her voice. "And I didn't have a flashlight; all I could see is what my headlights showed. I didn't see anything about what happened to him.''

"Do you think he was murdered?''

"Yes.''

"Any idea why?''

"None at all.''

"Could it have been something to do with a client?''

"I didn't know anything about his practice. We only had a couple of days together a year; we didn't talk shop. If he represented criminals, they may have decided to get rid of him. It's possible; I don't know.''

"Did you go back to LA afterward?''

"Yes, but just to settle things up. Just for a couple of days. My mom took it very badly—she was sure right from the start that Dan was dead. And with Dad gone, there was no one for her to turn to. I decided it was time for me to be closer to home. So I quit my job and moved back.''

"Where are you working now?''

"For a small company. Up near Pottsville. I'm the office manager.''

"Not nursing?''

"Ten years as a scrub nurse is enough. And now all this HIV. I was ready for a career change anyway.''

"Listen, do you still have any of his things?''

"No. He had an apartment in Philly. Not in a very good section of town. Mom cleared it out before I came back from California.''

I glanced at the clock behind her and saw that it was after eight, late enough to call my source. I gave Lisa a missing persons questionnaire to fill out and sent her downstairs.

The phone rang at least ten times before he picked up. He said nothing.

"This is Garrett.''

"Where you callin' from?''

"Line's clean. Guaranteed. And no bugs in the room.''

"I like a nice clean room.''

"Need some news.''

"Need some cash.''

"I'm on a case; if the stuff is good, I can deliver."

"You understan', I gotta set the price."

"First you deliver. I don't pay to find out who's president."

"What's the case?"

"Lawyer named Daniel Wilson disappeared seven years ago. He was partners with a lawyer named Leo Strasnick. Here in town. The way Wilson disappeared, it could have been a hit. But there's no body."

"You want me to find out if there was a hit? Out of my league, baby. Folks askin' questions like that don't ask long."

"Just find out if Wilson, or Strasnick, was tied to any organization. Or in any trouble. That'll be enough."

"Call me Tuesday noon."

"I need the score by tomorrow."

"Tomorrow? Baby, don't bust my chops!"

"No bullshit, man."

He sighed. "Check back tomorrow afternoon, late. Let it ring twice and then call back." He hung up.

I retrieved Lisa from downstairs and made a show of reviewing the form. She had dutifully filled in the names and addresses of several possible leads. Her skin was pale and contrasted with her dark eyes. She had small gold earrings in each ear.

"Were you satisfied with the police, Miss Wilson?"

"I was used to Los Angeles; they seemed a little backward. But they were very thorough. And they wanted to solve the case. They checked into every angle.''

''Including you.''

''Yes. I was shocked at first, but then they explained that I had to be eliminated as a suspect before they could go any further. It made sense to me.'' She paused. ''I want to tell you that I feel very—privileged—to have you working on this case. I can see you're good and that you're working hard already.''

''Well, thank you.'' It always made me nervous to get complimented during a case, even by a client who wasn't a suspect. ''And thank you for your help. You've given me a lot of leads to run down—and there's not much time to do it in. Now, where can you be reached?''

''My address and phone are on the form, but I'm not sure if I'm going home or not before the hearing. If I'm not there I'll be with my mom. It's on there, too.''

''Will you be at your mom's the rest of the day today?''

''I have a couple of errands this morning; then I'll be there.''

''Would it be convenient to interview your mom around five o'clock?''

''I don't think you'll find she's much help. She doesn't know anything.''

''Most of what I do isn't finding things out; it's eliminating certain possibilities.''

''She'll be home if I tell her.''

''Thanks. Say that it won't take long. Thanks again for your help.''

Taking the hint, she stood up. As she put on her

coat her breasts strained against the fabric of the sweater. When I'd finished locking up again and walking her to her car—not a mere courtesy in that neighborhood—she shook my hand again.

Her car had just pulled out into the stream of morning traffic when I saw a man in his late twenties about fifty feet away walking slowly toward me. He was wearing a hat and an expensive-looking topcoat over a suit and tie, which made him conspicuous enough. But mainly my attention was drawn to him because he was clearly interested in me. Both his hands were in his pockets, even though I could see the tops of gloves at his wrists.

I slowly turned around; another man, similarly dressed but a bit older, was walking toward me from the other direction. His hands were in his pockets, too. And just behind him was a cream Ford Taurus with multiple antennas on the roof.

Backing up until my back was against my building, I put my own hands in the pockets of my overcoat and found a pocket comb. I inched it forward between my forefinger and index finger until it created a bulge in my pocket. And then I waited; there was nothing else to do.

The older man came within five feet and stopped; the other stayed about ten feet away, well to one side. They were pros. There was no way I could have had a shot at both, and the older man wouldn't block the shot of the man behind.

"Come with us, buddy," said the older one. The voice was polite but absolutely flat.

"What if I don't want to?"

"Nobody asked you."

"Oh?"

"You can go in one piece or a couple. All the same to us."

I believed him absolutely. "Where are we going?"

"Just get in. If we wanted you out, you'd be out already." That was my own reasoning, too. "Okay," I said. "Lead the way."

We got into the Ford, with the younger man driving, the older man in the left-hand backseat, and me in the right backseat. As we drove, the older man frisked me, briefly but thoroughly. He hesitated when he found the comb and looked me in the eye. His look seemed to say that if he was the kind of man who smiled, this would have been worth smiling about. But he wasn't and he didn't. Then he took out a black box with an antenna; it looked like a walkie-talkie, but I knew it was an FM receiver set to some very special frequencies. He turned it on, sliding through the bands very slowly, waiting for a sign that I was carrying a concealed transmitter. A gun they understood; they probably thought it was as normal as carrying a comb. But a wire was different. If the radio went off, there was a fair chance they would kill me right there. I was very thankful that it didn't.

We made some turns, got onto Lancaster Avenue, and headed east in light traffic. We crossed over the Schuylkill on Vine, made a right at Sixteenth, and parked in front of a small office building near Pine. No one said a word during the drive.

They escorted me into the building. The younger one took me up to the third floor and directed me to a blank door at the end of the hall. The older one stayed downstairs, presumably watching the stairwell and fire escape. The thought of running never occurred to me; when they caught up to me, and it could only be a matter of *when* and not *if*, they would break both my legs and consider it a mild admonition.

The door opened into an office, bare except for a metal desk and two chairs. Some phones, boxes, and coils of cable took up one corner; the room was clearly not in regular use.

A slender man in his late fifties was sitting behind the desk. When I came in he was looking down, puzzling over some documents on legal-size paper. After a moment, he put the papers in a drawer and stood up. His hair was mostly gray and cropped very short. He kept his chin down, his shoulders back, and his feel slightly apart, giving him a military bearing. He had the look of a man who gave and took orders without discussion. But whatever kinds of orders he dealt in, they were important ones; his suit looked like it hadn't left the store for less than a grand. Strasnick was starting to look ordinary by comparison. "Mr. Garrett, so glad you could come."

His handshake, like his voice, was hard, powerful, and dry. I was relieved when he let go, as if I'd gotten free of a live electric wire. "Please sit down, Mr. Garrett. First of all, let me apologize for the unfortunate events of this morning. I trust you appreciate that it couldn't be helped under the circumstances. As you well know, we are both working under a great time pressure. Sometimes normal courtesies must be dispensed with. Yes. I'm sure you understand. Now allow me to play host. Would you care for some coffee?"

"Okay." I didn't trust my voice with anything more.

"How do you take it?"

"Black."

He pressed a tiny button on the side of the desk and leaned slightly toward it. "Joseph, two coffees, one black."

"Did you like New York?"

He simply raised his eyebrows, questioning.

"That's the way you order coffee there. It comes with cream unless you say black."

He smiled, the way a skull or a shark smiles. "Very observant, Mr. Garrett. I've been here for some years now. But to answer your question, yes, I found the city very enjoyable."

A man entered through a side door carrying a small tray with two Styrofoam cups. His suit jacket was off and he was wearing a shoulder holster with a 9mm Beretta, one of the new double-action automatics with a magazine capacity of fourteen rounds. And under his other armpit he carried two spare magazines. His right trouser leg didn't hang smoothly; I figured he had a second gun stashed in an ankle holster. Joseph was not a man to mess with unless you had an infantry platoon backing you up; nor was the man in front of me.

Joseph withdrew; neither of us touched our cups. "Mr. Garrett, like yourself I am an attorney. I am house counsel for various business interests in New Jersey and Pennsylvania. As you might imagine, the duties of house counsel are somewhat less defined than those of an outside attorney. I am called upon to give counsel and assist my clients regarding many varied situations, as you are."

"Were."

He frowned and nodded in sympathy. For a moment he had me believing that he was sincerely concerned. But his eyes betrayed him. They were as cold and hard as the muzzles of .45s. I wondered how many times he'd ordered men killed; I took it for granted that he had. Sometimes as we talked he seemed to see me. Other times he looked right through me, as if his mind were elsewhere. At that moment I wasn't there for him. "Yes, yes, I understand that the state supreme court was closely divided on your case. True?"

"Five votes for suspension, four for censure only."

"So sad, to be so close to success and have it slip away. Tell me, did you file for reconsideration?"

I wondered where the conversation was going. "For what it's worth. The review petition doesn't keep the license suspension from going into effect. And they can sit on it for as long as they want. Or never rule at all. They've been sitting on it for two years already. From what my attorney tells me, in some of these cases they never act on petitions for reconsideration at all."

"Does your attorney have influence with the court?"

"He's a specialist in supreme court appeals; he's very knowledgeable about the personalities on the court and how they're likely to react."

He waved his hand in a small dismissive gesture. "No, any good technician can do that. I mean *influence.*"

"No."

"Perhaps if someone would intercede on your behalf, behind the scenes, as it were. You only need one vote. And besides, even among the majority, there may be a feeling that now you've suffered enough."

It took a few seconds for the implications of his statement to sink in. They could even swing the vote of one—or more—state supreme court justices? Even though the room was well heated, I put my hands around the coffee cup to keep warm. I tried to keep my voice level.

"What do you have in mind?"

"It has been brought to my attention that you're investigating the disappearance of one Daniel Wilson."

"That's correct." Technically, this was a breach of my duty of confidentiality. Under the circumstances, I didn't care. Playing stupid with this man could conflict with another duty the investigator owes the client—staying alive to see the case through.

"Concern has been expressed," he said slowly, measuring out his words, "about the appropriateness of such an inquiry."

"I'm not trying to find who killed him."

"Oh? Then what is your concern?"

"Simply to establish that he is dead. Are you familiar with the presumption of death arising from an absence of seven years?"

"Oh, yes. So your inquiry is part of a civil action, relating to his estate?"

"Yes. The hearing is Monday afternoon in Montgomery County, in the Orphan's Court Division. The issue is whether a life insurance policy is payable.''

"Who is your client?"

"I'm working for Wilson's estate."

"But who, exactly?"

I decided I'd said enough. He didn't seem, somehow, to know as much as he pretended. "The estate itself is a legal entity. It's my client.''

He smiled again, and I began to sweat. "You know, it's useless to take such a position. We've had you under surveillance.''

He was temporizing; two could play. "I'm surprised you tipped your hand by picking me up. You could have followed me on my rounds today.''

"Come, come, Mr. Garrett. We knew last night you were conscious of us when you ran the tollbooth.''

"I spotted your people even earlier.'' I looked at my forearm; it was faint but still legible. "Pennsylvania registration TRD-two-three-eight?''

He was unimpressed. "Assuming that is the correct plate, in the first place, you could have noted the number this morning and guessed that it was the same vehicle as last night.''

"I was brought to the car from the front; Pennsylvania cars have only rear plates. And anyway, it wouldn't be written on my arm.''

He nodded. "Now just out of curiosity, why did you tip your hand and let us know you knew you were being followed? You forfeited an opportunity to sow false leads. Plus, you should have known it would force us to act.''

"I was near my house. I didn't know if you knew my identity or if you were just trailing me. I couldn't take the risk of taking them home if they didn't know who I was already.''

I was hoping he would tell me I'd guessed wrong, that they'd known my identity last night. Then I would have known that they'd been tipped off. The only people who'd known last night that I was on the case were Jon Franklin, Harry Ziemer, Leo Strasnick, and Mark Louchs. And maybe Lisa Wilson. But my luck wasn't running, or perhaps he saw the trap. ''And back to the subject under discussion,'' he continued. ''My clients are concerned about the reexamination of closed business. They have some instructions for you.''

''I'm listening.''

''You may stay on the Wilson case if you wish, but forgo any inquiries regarding the precise circumstances of his disappearance. To put it simply, go through the motions. The outcome of this civil case is of no concern to us. In return, we can advise you regarding the retention of a new appeals counsel to work with your present attorney. Someone who will be listened to when he speaks.''

''Or?''

''There is no 'or,' Mr. Garrett.''

''I have a proposal of my own.''

Something flickered across his face, something like amusement. ''Go ahead.''

I decided to ease into it slowly. ''It's safe to say that Mr. Wilson was not the victim of a natural catastrophe.''

''That would seem a reasonable inference.''

''More particularly, this was not random or accidental.''

''I would tend to agree.''

"Therefore, it happened for a reason."

"If it was not an accident, it would have to be deliberate."

I took a chance. I had nothing to lose, and I couldn't see walking away from this one. "Now, correct me if I'm wrong, but it would seem that there are two possible reasons for what happened. Either it was pure retaliation or it happened in the course of trying to acquire information."

"Go on."

"If it was retaliation, there's no service I can render. But if it wasn't . . ."

"You understand, I have no authority, and can obtain no authority, to discuss my client's affairs with you."

It was my turn to nod. "I don't want to know anything about them."

"Mr. Garrett, are you suggesting that my client hire you? I trust not."

"No. My proposal is simply that if I learn anything that would be of interest to you, I will pass it along."

"We have our own investigative resources."

"They haven't delivered in this case."

"Do you think you can do better?"

"What do you have to lose?"

"It would be much simpler to have you off the case. So much less risk." I couldn't tell if he meant my resignation or death. "You're out to prove Wilson was killed."

"By his own hand. Or by accident. Or by disease. Or by person or persons unknown. There is no evidence as to who did it and I'm not looking for any."

He frowned. "You seek to introduce complexities. I dislike them. You recall how Alexander dealt with the Gordian Knot?"

"I think the better analogy would be the myth of the Hydra."

"Ah, a man of classical learning." His voice brightened but his eyes looked past me again. He seemed to be interested, but also thinking of something else at the same time. "One of the labors of Hercules, was it not?"

"Yes. He had to kill the Hydra; a beast of many heads. When one was cut off, two grew back in its place."

"You're not suggesting that two investigators will come forward if you are removed from the case?"

"Nothing so direct. But what we have now is a seven-year-old disappearance with no leads. No one's cared about it in years, and once I'm through with the case on Monday, no one ever will again. But if something happens to me while I'm working this case, the police will get interested—not only in my case, but in the one I was working on."

He considered my point for a moment. "Mr. Garrett, I am going to take it upon myself to deviate slightly from my instructions. I'm told that when you were in practice, you had a high reputation for reliability. I am prepared to take you at your word, for the moment. I will tell you this, and no more. Do not ask anything further. We are seeking the return of certain property. It is believe to have last been in the hands of Mr. Wilson. If your inquiries lead to recovery of the property, then my deviation from instructions will be forgiven. If you cannot recover the property, or if your conduct creates other difficulties, I will have no choice but to take appropriate measures.'' He sounded as if he really didn't care how it turned out. He handed me a business card with nothing but five phone numbers printed on it. ''I will be available this weekend at either of the bottom two; one is my cellular phone. Don't photocopy the card or write the numbers down anywhere else. And don't lose the card; all of the numbers are confidential.''

My mouth was dry and I wanted a sip of coffee, but I was afraid my hands were shaking too badly to pick up the cup. I took the card without comment and put it in my jacket pocket.

''Good luck to you, Mr. Garrett.'' He didn't look up when I opened the door.

5

SATURDAY, 1:00 P.M.

I caught a bus back to my office and looked at the information Lisa had left. Mainly I was interested in Wilson's best friend, Todd Brogan, and his former girlfriend, then Elizabeth Chatwin, now Elizabeth Dosterburg. I was able to reach both of them by phone. Todd lived only forty minutes away, in West Chester. He sounded pleased to cooperate, but said that Sunday afternoon would be better because his oldest boy had a swimming practice starting at noon. We agreed on late Sunday afternoon at his home. Mrs. Dosterburg said she was available anytime; since she was further away, in Hanover, I decided to see her immediately.

The turnpike would have been a few minutes faster, but I decided to go the long way, on 30. I always enjoyed the countryside, even with all the leaves down and a few inches of snow. Especially Lancaster County. Chester County is well on the way to being one big Philadelphia suburb, and somehow I'd never cared for York County. But Lancaster—there was always something to see. Forty miles of rolling hills, some with just farmhouses, some with little towns, and patches of woods in between. At one time the whole county had been forested; I was sorry I'd missed seeing it.

Hanover was a quiet town of red-brick houses about fifteen miles from Gettysburg on a road that led nowhere. You only go to Hanover if you intend to. Her house was in the middle of a street of identical two-story row houses, each with a second-floor bay window. The street was well tended; the paint was fresh and many of the houses had white window boxes. Most of the houses looked like owner-occupieds, but there was also the inevitable beauty shop, a bar, and a corner mom-and-pop grocery.

I left my car across the street, not bothering to lock it. This was the sort of neighborhood where you didn't need to. There weren't many left, and I liked the feeling.

"Mr. Garrett?" a thin, high voice called from her door. "Please come right in."

She was a plump, pleasant-faced woman in her middle thirties with blond hair cut too short and with too much jewelry. She was wearing a pink silk blouse with a high V neck that probably had looked better twenty pounds ago, and a black skirt, almost new, that was more in line with her present proportions. She showed me into the front sitting room. With something that was halfway between a wave and a curtsy she invited me to sit on the sofa.

"Can I get you some coffee? Some tea?"

I'd learned to accept anything offered; if nothing else, consuming it gave you an excuse to prolong the interview. "Coffee would be fine," I said, matching her measured tone. "It's quite cold outside."

"Yes." She nodded at me again and disappeared through a door to the back. I noticed she was wearing high heels.

While she was out of the room I got up and looked around. The furniture was obviously from somewhere else. It was old, in fine condition, but it was too big for the room; chairs were jammed against the sofa, the Oriental was tucked under at one end, and the side table almost touched the wall. Inherited, I decided. Like its owner, the house was trying to live just above its station. On the mantel was her wedding picture, showing a thinner and prettier Elizabeth, with a long blond mane, smiling at the camera, next to a thin, dark young man in a white tuxedo. He didn't seem to be smiling. I wonder if he'd suspected what was in store.

Before I could poke around any further she was back, carefully holding a silver tray in both hands. She moved as if it were a religious relic—which in a sense it probably was. She'd been busy since I called. In addition to a silver coffeepot, with matching silver sugar bowl and creamer, the tray contained two cups, spoons, cloth napkins, and an assortment of small pastries.

"Thank you very much. I appreciate your hospitality." I'd gulped two cheeseburgers and a large order of fries in York half an hour ago, but I took the coffee and a couple of pastries. No point in being difficult.

"You're very welcome, Mr. Garrett."

"I also appreciate your seeing me on such short notice."

She nodded. "Your time must be very precious right now. I'll try not to take up too much. But before we start, just how can I help? I didn't see him for months before he vanished."

"Yes, I know. It's a matter of negative evidence as much as anything—"

"Negative evidence?"

"Sorry, that's really more of a legal term. What I mean is, this is a case of a disappearance. If a person disappears and is not heard from for a long enough time, the law presumes he's dead. So evidence that something didn't happen—that you didn't hear from him, and that none of your mutual friends did—is important."

"I see," she murmured. I could tell from her look that she didn't, but at least it gave me a chance to start.

"How did you meet?"

"At work. I had just been graduated from business college and I was working in Philadelphia as a legal assistant. My firm was in the same building as Daniel's."

"And when was that?"

"I thought you would ask that so I looked it up. It was just before Thanksgiving, eight years ago."

"So you two knew each other for a little more than a year before he disappeared?"

"Yes and no. We started dating within a few weeks, and we were serious by January. But we broke up that summer; it was August, not long before Labor Day."

"You have quite a memory."

"No, I have it all written down. And the date of our breaking up is in my mind anyway. We were going to use the Labor Day weekend to drive around and look at restaurants and reception halls for our wedding.''

"I see. I'm sorry; I didn't realize that things had been that serious.''

"That's quite all right. It's been a long time. And I'm married now, of course,'' she added in obvious afterthought. She looked down at her wedding ring as if she'd just seen it for the first time. "The engagement hadn't been formally announced anyway, and there wasn't a ring. It was more like something that we both based our plans on.''

"You mentioned you were looking up dates and things. Is there a diary?''

She shook her head. "Oh, no. I just keep my old appointment books. From when I was a legal assistant. I would write in things like if we had a date, where we went, if we saw a movie what the movie was, things like that. Nothing more at all.''

There was a diary, but I could probably pull out her fingernails before she'd let me see it. And anyway, as long as she was answering my questions, it probably didn't matter. I didn't want to know all her girlish fantasies about marrying Daniel. "Tell me about him.''

"He was a really wonderful person. Always polite, attentive, a perfect gentleman. Very intelligent, well-read, well-traveled. But not arrogant; he could always laugh at himself.''

"I've heard it said that he was depressed.''

"At times. More toward the end. He had his moods. He could be very withdrawn, and he wouldn't tell me what he was thinking. But he never lost his temper or took it out on me.''

"You say he seemed more down later in your relationship?"

"Very much so. At first he seemed so bouncy, so cheerful. You could see it in his eyes. But as the months went by he started to brood. His moods would pass and for a few days, even a few weeks, he'd be his old self. Then they would start again. By the end he was down all the time."

"What was he worrying about?"

She met his eyes. "Mr. Garrett, I never had the slightest idea then and I don't know. I wish I did; perhaps I could have helped. I only know that he was terribly bothered by something. I pestered him to tell me, even more toward the end. I thought if we were going to be married he should share everything with me, that we shouldn't keep secrets. But he never said."

"Ma'am, there are certain categories that most worries fall into. Would you mind helping me get to the bottom of this, if I can?"

"Sure."

"Could it have been money?"

"No. He managed his money very well, from what I could see. He was very generous with me, buying me clothes and jewelry and taking me out to dinner. He treated me like a queen. But he was very frugal with himself. I only saw his apartment a few times; it was very—basic, shall I say. We never stayed overnight there, and that was fine with me. It was much less than he could have afforded. He'd worked his way through school, so he had no school loans to repay. He once said he had enough money saved up to put a down payment on a house for us plus buy the furniture."

"Did he say where the money was?"

"Funny you should ask that. He was very odd about banks. He told me readily enough about his finances; he volunteered everything I've just told you. But as far as where he kept his money, he wasn't very sophisticated. He kept it in cash in a safe-deposit box."

"Did he say why?"

"It wasn't not trusting banks—if he didn't he could have buried it somewhere, I suppose. He just didn't like people tracing what he did through his money. Tracing how he spent it, I mean."

"Do you know what he meant by that?"

"Not a clue. Except that he talked about it in a peculiar way. Not about how he'd spent it in the past, but how he was going to spend it in the future."

"Nothing more specific?"

"Well, he'd say, 'If I wanted to do something that cost money, I wouldn't want everybody knowing about it.' Does that make any sense to you?"

"Only if I had an idea of what he was going to spend money on."

"It didn't come up often; it was his money and we never got to the point of pooling our resources. Until we were ready to set a date, it wasn't my place to ask."

"Did he gamble?"

"Not at all. He said that trying cases was gambling enough. And he said that money easily come by would go just as easily. Or even that it could bring back luck. We went to Atlantic City once; he let me go into the casino and he took a walk on the beach."

"Let me ask about some other things. Did he have a drinking problem?"

"He was a hard drinker, you might say; most of the trial attorneys I've met are. He had a couple of drinks every night after work to relax—Scotch, mainly. On weekend evenings he might have a third drink. Or we might have a bottle of wine with dinner. But if we had the wine, he wouldn't order a drink, too. He never used eating as an excuse to sneak more alcohol." She allowed herself a sad, rueful smile and tilted her head a bit, remembering. "I'm sorry, you must think that I spent a year cataloguing his personal habits. But when you're thinking of marriage you keep an eye out for such things. Anyway, he never drank anything during the day, even on weekends. And I can't say that I ever saw him drunk. He used it to relax, nothing more. And because it was part of the image."

"Image?"

"Being a litigator, a gunslinger, as they say. Being tough. Like being a Marine or a paratrooper—he told me a story once about that; he said it was a true story. I think it described him well. Do you want to hear it?"

"Please."

She pursed her lips. "I want to be sure I get this right. It was just before D day, in World War Two. General Eisenhower is reviewing the parachute soldiers who are supposed to jump behind enemy lines. They're all big, strapping men, covered with camouflage paint and carrying their equipment; rifles and ammunition and such. He walks down the line and comes to a puny little fellow with glasses. He's almost buried under his pack and rifle and everything. General Eisenhower looks at him and says, 'Son, do you enjoy jumping out of airplanes?' 'No, sir.' 'Then why do you do it?' 'Because I like being around men who do.' '' We both smiled. ''He told me that story once at a dinner party and one of the men thought it was a homosexual joke. It was one of the few times I ever saw him angry. I'm not going to repeat what he said—he used some words that night I didn't think he knew—but the essence was, it's not a story about sexual preference, it's about courage. About getting through difficult things.''

''This is a difficult question, and I don't want to embarrass you, but since the subject has come up . . .''

She pursed her lips and took her time answering; I wasn't sure if she was thinking about how to phrase it, or just remembering. ''Dan was no caveman, Mr. Garrett. He was a gentle, considerate lover. He wasn't the kind of man who would ravish you at first sight.'' For just an instant she flicked her eyes at me. ''But if he had a little encouragement, if he felt secure, he was fine.''

''Thank you. It's hard to discuss these matters with a total stranger.''

''I don't feel that way toward you, Mr. Garrett. I find it very easy to talk to you, as a matter of fact. I'm very much at ease.''

I nodded.

''By the way, since we're speaking about sex, can I tell you something?''

''Please.''

''He liked photography. Portraits. He had a couple of very nice cameras and some indoor lighting equipment. He kept everything at my place. He loved taking pictures of me.'' A smile began to form and she looked away, just a little.

''Pictures?''

''Oh, nothing X-rated. But R, if you know what I mean. I'd be wearing lingerie or a pair of stockings. Or nothing at all. Very nicely done, with soft focus and pretty lighting. He had a real gift; he made me look so glamorous. I told him he could have been a photographer for *Playboy*. He just laughed.'' She played with her wedding ring.

''Did he ever sell any of the photographs commercially?''

''Lord, I don't think so. That certainly wasn't the idea. It was private, just for us. Just think of all those men looking at me.'' Her voice trailed off and she fingered the top button of her blouse. ''When we broke up he gave me back the pictures. He said he didn't keep any. Later my husband made me throw them away.'' For a moment a sour expression crossed her face, then it was gone.

''That shoots down a theory I was working on.''

''Oh?''

''That he might have been gay, and keeping it in the closet; that somebody was trying to blackmail him.''

She laughed. ''If you saw him on the street you might have thought that, just by looking. He was a . . . mild-looking man. But no, he certainly wasn't gay.''

''I'd like to ask you about the photography some more. Did he sell other pictures? Or do work for people as a photographer?'' Maybe he'd taken a picture, or seen something, he shouldn't have.

She shook her head and dropped her hand to her lap. "No, not that I know of. It was just a private hobby."

"Did he like being a lawyer?"

"Oh, yes. But he was willing to admit that he was scared before starting a trial. Most trial lawyers don't talk about that. They love to talk about how they outsmarted the other side, or how they worked hard and found new evidence, but they never talk about being scared. Not everyone likes being reminded."

"All right, then. Did he take any drugs?"

"He'd smoked marijuana in college, but he stopped when he got to law school. He said it made him feel too dopey. There was never a suggestion that he took anything else. We were only together a couple of times all weekend but I'm sure I would have noticed."

"He didn't usually stay with you on weekends?"

"No, we used to fight about that, as a matter of fact. He'd spend every spare minute he could with me Monday through Friday, but most weekends he liked to be by himself. I told him that I felt like a weekend widow, and we weren't even married."

"What did he do?"

"He said he was traveling. But he never took me along."

"What do you think?"

"Well, he was never home; I checked on that. But where he went, or if he was alone, I don't know."

"Could there have been another woman?"

"I've thought about that over the years, of course. But he told me I was the first woman he'd dated in more than a year. If there was someone else, I never had a clue.''

''I talked to a neighbor who said he used to see a blond woman, well-dressed, around the place. Not all the time, but both before and during the time you two went out.''

She was quiet, and then she shook her head. ''He practically lived with me during the week. I can't see how there could have been time for anything serious, unless she was out of town somewhere. When things got bad I asked him if there was another woman; I told him he should be honest with me. He swore that there wasn't.''

''Do you have any idea who the blonde was?''

''Are you sure you're not thinking of his sister?''

''She's not blonde. I met her this morning.''

''Not naturally. But Dan kidded her once, when the three of us were together, about how she'd gone to LA and turned into a blonde. I guess she must be a brunette again now.''

''Did he talk about his family much?''

''Talk about them? Oh, yes. We saw his mom almost every week. They were very close; and when Lisa was in town he'd take off a couple of days to visit with her. I liked Lisa, but I never got to know her very well. She only visited twice when Dan and I were together, and she and Dan spent some of the time together without me. But it always seemed like a happy family to me. His mother was very proud of both of them.''

''Did he have many friends?''

''A few, but they were good friends. The kind of people you could always count on.''

"Can you remember any of them?"

"The only one whose name I recall is Todd Brogan. He used to live in West Chester. I can't remember his wife's name, but they were a very nice
couple." She hesitated. "Dan must have decided
that things weren't going to work out months before
it ended. He stopped introducing me to his friends
pretty early on."

"Why didn't it work out?"

"I don't know. He was so happy at first, and then
it seemed that our being together was an effort for
him; and then he sort of gave up trying. We went
along a while longer and then it ended."

"But I thought you said you were looking for
places for a wedding reception."

"I was; he wasn't. I could feel him slipping
away, you see. And I loved him. I really did. I
thought that by pressing for marriage I could put
some momentum in things. He went along, but his
heart wasn't in it. The next week I got the letter."

"Letter?"

"Telling me it was over."

"What did he say?"

"Would you like to see it?"

"Please."

She went upstairs and returned with a small white
envelope. Our fingertips brushed as I accepted it. I
could feel her eyes on mine, cool and appraising.
I saw that the top button of her blouse was undone.

The letter was handwritten on plain ivory statio-
nery. The writing was small, regular, and clear. It
looked familiar. I wondered where I'd seen a sample of his handwriting.

Dear Liz,

I'm terribly sorry, but it's over. I've come to realize that this just isn't going to work out. It's not
anyone's fault, least of all yours. But it's time to
face the truth. I have to do things that don't involve
you or anyone other than myself. And if you have
a chance for happiness with Bill I don't want to
stand in your way.

I'm grateful for the fun we had together. You'll
always be remembered with fondness.

Love,
Dan

I handed it back. "Did you speak to him about
this afterward?"

"Yes, but it didn't add anything. This is as much
as I know."

"You say this was about four months before he
disappeared?"

She nodded.

"Did he contact you again after this letter?"

"No. I phoned him after I got it. We talked one
time. That was all."

"Who's Bill?"

"My husband. We were married the June after
Dan disappeared."

"You were seeing him and Dan at the same
time?"

"There wasn't anything physical till after Dan
and I broke up." She leaned back in her chair and
a little sideways; I wasn't sure if she was getting
more comfortable or looking for a position to show
her breasts to the best advantage. "I didn't know
everything about Dan, but I was afraid for a long

time before it ended that it wasn't going anywhere.''

"Dan knew about Bill.''

"I told him. I wasn't going to try to keep it a secret.''

"Did you have a fight about it? Was that what led to your breaking up?''

"Not really a fight. He took it well; too well, if you ask me.''

"It didn't make him jealous?''

"I was hoping it would make him see that it was a danger sign, that we were drifting apart. But he just said, 'fine, if that's the way you want it.' That's when I was sure it wasn't going to work.''

"You're aware of the circumstances of his disappearance?''

"Oh, yes. The police questioned me at the time, as a matter of fact.''

"Are you in touch with his family or any of his old friends?''

"No. We really didn't have any mutual friends, they were either mine or his. As far as family I went to his mother's house; no one would answer the door. But I think she was home. Then I wrote to Lisa and to his mother, expressing my concern. I received a reply from his mother thanking me That's been it.''

"And you haven't heard from him since he disappeared?''

"No.''

"You've moved and changed your name; if he wanted to get in touch with you, would he know how to do it?''

"Oh, yes. If he called my old office, anyone there

could tell him where I am. Or if he called my parents.''

"Do you have an opinion?"

"He had a good deal of money in cash. He was very unhappy; not because of breaking up with me, I hope, but you can tell by the letter he wasn't cheerful. His possessions in his apartment weren't worth much. He had little to lose. He knew a lot about criminal law, how investigations work. He knew what they would look for.''

"You think he decided to disappear.''

"I feel certain of that. To me, the only question is why.''

I stood up. "Thank you for your hospitality. And if I find out, I'll certainly let you know.''

She put her hand lightly on my forearm as we reached the door. "I appreciate that your schedule is tight just now. And if you'd like to call again feel free to do so.''

"The case will be over, one way or the other, on Monday.''

"No matter.''

I'd been propositioned a few times in my life, but never so elegantly. But Mrs. Dosterburg wasn't for me. Even if she lost forty pounds and grew out her hair. There wouldn't be enough room in bed for her and me and all her dreams.

"I won't forget that. Oh, and one more thing,'' I said as I put on my coat, "You mentioned that Daniel knew a lot about—how did you put it?—criminal law and investigations?''

"Oh, yes. That was most of what he did. He wouldn't talk about it much, and I respected the confidentiality, but he did a lot of work on high-level drug cases. And white-collar crime. I'm sure you know what I mean.''

''Was that what he always did?''

''Not when he started practice, I don't think. But when I knew him.''

I hadn't been on the case twenty-four hours and already I'd been lied to. Suddenly Mrs. Dosterburg and the touch of her hand seemed a long way away. ''Thank you very much. And now I have to run. I have to see someone in Philadelphia right away.''

She said something more, but I was already crossing the street.

6

SATURDAY, 3:00 P.M.

Strasnick's house was what I expected, an elegant turn-of-the-century mansion on the Main Line with a long driveway to insulate the owners from the madding crowd. I wasn't expecting two matching new black Mercedes sedans in the driveway or that the door would be answered by a maid. At least she wasn't black or wearing a uniform; even ostentation has to stop somewhere.

No one had answered when I'd called his office. Finding him at home was a calculated risk. And as good as any, since I had no place else to look.

The maid showed me through a white-tiled foyer to the rear of the house, knocked on an oak door, and withdrew, taking my overcoat with her.

"Come in."

The room was small, but paneled in oak to match the door. There were no windows. The brass chandelier above my head was turned off; a small brass reading light on the desk threw a pool of light on a scattering of documents. Strasnick looked up at me over his reading glasses. He was wearing a dress shirt and a tie, but the collar was open and the tie pulled down.

"You're working hard, Mr. Garrett."

"So are you."

"It goes with the practice, as you know. Never enough hours in the day."

I sat down. He regarded me from across the desk. "What can I do for you today, Mr. Garrett?"

"Tell me the truth."

He didn't blink. "Concerning?"

"The nature of Wilson's practice."

"I thought I'd already made that clear."

I tried to keep the anger out of my voice. "And what was your understanding of what you told me?"

"General practice, with an emphasis on trial work," he explained patiently.

"Not criminal?"

"A few DUIs."

"And how that differs from your practice now?"

"Mainly in that we can afford to be more selective in our choice of clients. I thought it was a simple enough explanation."

"Mr. Strasnick, I know a lot of attorneys in this area. I know a lot of people that did private criminal work seven years ago. As a matter of fact, I know several people who were assistant district attorneys back then. I can very easily find out exactly what kind of trial practice Wilson had. I'd prefer to have you tell me yourself."

"I trust you're not threatening me, Mr. Garrett."

"No."

"Or thinking that I had some role in his disappearance."

"No."

He stood up. "Then I will have to ask you to leave. You are not my client, I have no obligation to talk to you, and I have nothing more to say. The maid will see you out."

I stayed sitting down. "I have it on very good authority that at the time he disappeared his practice was almost exclusively organized crime. Are we going to talk or do I have you subpoenaed to testify about that on Monday?"

"What do you mean, subpoenaed? I'm not under suspicion."

"No, but with the circumstances surrounding his disappearance, I'm sure the judge would find it highly relevant that he—and his firm—had ties to the mob." I stood up; two could play at that game. "The hearing's at one-thirty in Montgomery County Common Pleas. I'm not sure of the courtroom; it'll be on the subpoena. Oh, and if Monday doesn't suit you, if you can't make it, no problem; we'll get it reset for your convenience. After all, you're a key witness." I started for the door.

"Mr. Garrett, please sit down."

I stopped near the door but didn't turn around.

His voice was soft and measured. "I can see we need to discuss this further."

I sat back down and waited. He leaned back in his swivel chair and pressed his fingertips together. "This is going to take a while to explain. Want a cup of coffee? Or something to eat?"

"No, thanks."

"Look, Dave—can I call you that? I hear you used to be a lawyer yourself."

"News travels fast."

"Stories like yours do. I remember reading about

it at the time. It's the kind of thing that sticks in your mind. But I didn't realize it was you yesterday. One of my associates made the connection.'' I wondered where this was going. ''Tell me, what sort of practice did you have?''

''At the end, mostly personal injury.''

''Were you with a firm?''

''Yes.''

''Did you start out with that firm?''

''No, I clerked for a judge for a year, then hung out my own shingle.''

''In Philadelphia?''

I nodded.

''How long were you on your own?''

''Two-and-a-half years. Then my firm took me on as an associate.''

''I don't mean to pry, but if your early days were like ours, was it rough going at first?''

''If you mean did I nearly go broke, yes.''

''Hard to find clients, right?''

''Of course. Even then, there were ten thousand lawyers in the city.''

''And did you do any criminal work?''

''The first year it was nearly all criminal. Then it started to diversify a little.''

''Dan and I went through the same struggle, more recently than you.''

''Okay.''

''Let me guess how it was and you tell me if I'm wrong. You're a brand-new lawyer. Lots of expenses. You have no particular expertise yet, no speciality. Neither a claimant nor an insurance carrier will hire you for civil lawsuits because you have no trial experience. The clientele you attract is mainly criminal matters. Correct so far?''

"Yes."

"And the typical criminal client is a lousy credit risk. He has no money for a serious retainer. He's probably unemployed and already having trouble meeting his child support obligations. So you take the case with a two-hundred-dollar retainer, or even a hundred, and hope he'll come up with the rest. Promises and promises, sometimes a few dollars when a court appearance is at hand. Once the case is over, your claim for a fee is a total write-off, no matter how hard you try to collect.''

"Correct."

"It was the same way for Dan and me."

"Go on."

"How did you solve your problem?" he asked.

"As I got trial experience I was able to diversify a little. Some domestic, some landlord-tenant. Enough to get by. And then I got my offer with the firm.''

"Suppose that during that difficult first couple of years a client had come in on a criminal matter. A different sort of client than you'd ever seen. Older than the kids you normally represented, better dressed, with a—shall we say *complex*—criminal record. He says he needs to beat the charge very badly and wants your firm because he's heard you have the talent. He puts a cash retainer on the table that's as much money as the firm has taken in during the last two months. He says he'll pay more for a good result. And when your partner—Dan—gets the result, he doubles the retainer in gratitude.''

"You must have known what you were getting into.''

"Not right away. We just thought we'd been lucky. But suppose you were in this situation and in the months that followed, you got a stream of referrals from this man, people who were willing to pay almost any fee for good results, and who would give huge retainers anyway? Suppose your firm's income went up tenfold in six months?"

"They bought you and paid for you."

He shook his head. "No, you don't understand. There was never a contact with—what shall I call it?—the referring organization. Just individuals showing up by themselves. We never learned anything about how we were selected for the first client or how, exactly, they decided to keep sending people to us. And it was never homicides; all narcotics, RICO, embezzlement, extortion, arson, some prostitution, things of that nature."

"What would Dan have known?"

"Exactly what I have told you, no more. The clients never discussed anything but the facts of the case with us, not a one. It was better for everyone that way. There was never any one case that screamed out 'organized crime.' Nothing but the sheer number of cases. And there were never any big publicity cases; neither Dan nor I was ever in the newspapers. Everybody wanted it quiet, and it stayed that way."

"Who did the work?"

"We both did, at first. Then the firm started to diversify, just like you did. I handled the new matters and he concentrated on servicing the criminal clients. And very successfully, too, I might add."

"Was he ever threatened by a client?"

"No. Not, at least, that he told me. I'm sure he would have said something."

"Or by anyone on a client's behalf?"

"No. I told you, there was no contact. And besides, the people we were dealing with, both directly and indirectly, had realistic expectations. If you could win an acquittal or a favorable plea bargain, they were very happy. If there were no deals to be made and the case went against them, they were at least satisfied that he'd given them the best defense possible. We never heard a complaint. If they had been dissatisfied, the referrals would have stopped."

"At the time of his disappearance, what kinds of cases was he working on?"

"I reviewed this a few months ago, when I heard that there was going to be a hearing. I have it written down somewhere, but basically there was nothing out of the ordinary at the time. There were about fifty active files. Around ten were felony drug cases, another ten were misdemeanor drug cases, half a dozen each of assault, Uniform Firearms Act violations, RICO, and soliciting. The rest were a little of everything—a few divorces, custody, personal injury, even a zoning case."

"You told me the last time we met that he seemed dissatisfied. Is there anything you'd like to add now?"

He seemed puzzled by the question. "How do you mean?"

"Did he like the work?"

"Neither of us did, if you want my honest opinion. With the regular criminal trade, they may have been slow to pay, but they were usually poor souls of one sort or another; you could feel sorry for them. You hoped that if you got them off they would straighten themselves out. You could think that you were helping them get a second chance, sometimes. These people we're talking about—well, they didn't stir any of those emotions.''

''Did he want to quit?''

''At times, we both did.''

''What happened?''

''Each time we would talk about it and decide to hang in a little longer. The money allowed us to practice law on our other cases, just as we wanted. Take on interesting cases for free. We could turn away the ordinary cases we disliked. We could afford to hire associates. And we could afford to try the kind of cases we're discussing in the grand style. If we wanted to hire psychologists to help us pick jurors or fly in an expert from out of state or have expensive exhibits constructed, money was never an object. Just one example: in a drug case we might say that a certain toxicologist at the University of Illinois might be able to help us, and an envelope with five thousand in cash would be delivered the next day.''

''Were you afraid to quit, back then?''

He shook his head. ''I wish I could say that we kept trying to quit but were forced to continue, but it wouldn't be true. We discussed quitting but we never tried, at least when Dan was around. We decided that our imaginations were getting away from us if we thought they would compel us to take cases we didn't want. And that turned out to be true. They wanted good representation, but there was no reason it had to be us. There were lots of other hungry lawyers. Still are.''

"But you couldn't have known then that they would let you go so easily."

"No, we didn't. And frankly, Dan was never as convinced as I was that they would. Let me tell you what I told him. The organization went to great lengths never to deal with us directly. We never learned anything about them—we weren't privy to any trade secrets, as it were. That mean that they were deliberately keeping us at arm's length. I felt that it was of mutual benefit; they risked no secrets with us, we were not in a position to harm them. Ergo, we were no threat to them. If we left, no information went with us. They could afford to let us go."

"And?"

"We were right all along, as it turns out. After Dan disappeared I discussed the matter with the associates—there were no other partners then—and we decided to get out. We sent away the next three cases and we never heard from them again. My associates reported to me that a firm in Chester picked up the representation of all three."

"Why did Dan's disappearance make the difference?"

"It scared the hell out of us. First of all, assuming it was a homicide, we had no idea how it was connected with our organized crime representations. Or even if it was. We didn't know what to think. Was it a dissatisfied client from the organization? We'd never heard a complaint. Was it another client? Possibly. Could it be the organization itself? That didn't make much sense, because they kept right on sending us clients. But since everything we knew about them was guessing, nothing seemed out of the question. One of the associates even suggested that two groups were involved and that Dan had somehow been caught in the middle. It was as likely as anything else. The mere fact that we didn't know why was frightening. We felt we were really in over our heads. And if it wasn't a homicide, if it was some form of disappearance, well, that sent us a message, too. Whether it was a suicide or a charade to cover his running away, it told us about the stress involved in that kind of practice. With everything taken into account, we decided to get out.''

"What do you really think happened?''

"I'm sorry I lied to you about Dan, but I—well, let me explain it this way. You were a partner in a firm?''

"Yes.''

"Was it a close relationship with your partners?''

"With some of them, yes.''

"Then you'll know what I mean. You're with them eight, ten, twelve hours a day. You may not be on the same case, but you're always together. You see a lot more of them than you do your family. And they become like a family. Tell me, are you married?''

"Divorced.''

"Then I'll ask a different question. When you and your wife were in trouble, who did you tell first?''

"My partners.''

"Even before your family?''

I nodded.

"Dan was even more to me than an ordinary partner. We'd started it all together, sweated out meeting payroll, the whole thing. I was shocked when he left without telling me, but I respected his decision. And to be very candid, I wanted to protect him in this. I owe him a lot. I didn't want anyone trying to find him. So I hid his motive to disappear, and I told you I thought he was dead. I'm sorry I did that, but I hope you can appreciate my reasons.''

''So where is he?''

''I have no idea. Dave, let me tell you something else. I told you yesterday we were doing badly when he left. Obviously you know that wasn't true. He lived simply; he could have saved up money like crazy before he left. There would have been more than enough to travel on.''

''How much?''

''We took out the same. I was married, my wife didn't work, we had two small children. Even I was able to save something. Dan could have saved fifty thousand, maybe seventy-five. Enough to go to Arizona or Mexico or somewhere, take a low-visibility job, and not have to worry about money. At least for a long time.''

''Is there any evidence he's alive?''

''Nothing I'm aware of.''

''No word at all?''

''No. But that doesn't surprise me.''

''What do you mean? If you were that close.''

''He went to a lot of trouble to disappear in a way that would make them think he was dead. He must have felt, for whatever reason, that his life was in danger. It wouldn't be worth it to jeopardize his safety to let us know he's okay. If the situation were reversed, I'd keep my head down, too, and hope that my friends understood.''

"Has the insurance company subpoenaed you?"

"No. I told them I wouldn't be a cooperative witness."

"Why?"

"Because I really don't know what happened; it's just guesswork. The judge can do that as well as I. And because I don't want to get killed."

"Go on."

"The organization doesn't like publicity, especially publicity that suggests they were involved in murdering someone."

"Have you been threatened?"

"Not at all. They don't need to. It's obvious enough to me. And even if I'm wrong, I'm not going to take a chance. Even if this hearing results in the company having to pay the hundred thousand dollars when he's really not dead, I don't care—not when my life and the lives of my family are in the balance. If he's declared dead, then we get a check from the company and endorse it over to his estate. If he's not declared dead, there's no check for us to sign. It doesn't matter to me or my firm one way or the other."

I looked at my watch. I had covered a lot of ground, and I was already late for my appointment with Mrs. Wilson.

"Anything else you want to tell me?"

He grinned just a little. "Yes. If you run into Dan in the course of your investigation, please give him my best."

"I don't think I'm going to have the pleasure."

"No. Probably not." His smile disappeared. "Listen, I want to apologize about yesterday. It's not like me, and I didn't like doing it. I made a mistake about you."

"You could have saved me some time."

"If you were me, you'd have covered for your partner, too."

The maid retrieved my coat and let me out. It was warming, but the clouds threatened snow. I checked Mrs. Wilson's address and headed out. It may have been my imagination, but it seemed that the two Mercedes were happier once my Honda was gone.

Fortunately, the late afternoon traffic was light as I headed east. Wilson's mother lived in Overbrook, a section of the city that was too tough to die. Hemmed in by the slums of west Philadelphia on one side and by Saint Joseph's College, Saint Charles Seminary, and Lankenau Hospital on the other sides, it never gave up. The big brick houses never deteriorated into warrens of tiny apartments; instead, they were bought by yuppies and renovated. The apartment buildings never went co-op. The neighborhood stores stayed in business. It wasn't as pretty as it had once been, or as safe, but it was still a neighborhood.

Mrs. Wilson lived in a ground-floor brick apartment between a funeral home and a dry cleaner. When I knocked on her door, the peephole snapped open.

"Hi. I'm Dave Garrett, the investigator. I'm sorry I'm late. I'm here to talk about Dan's case."

The peephole shut but the door remained closed for at least half a minute. I heard two distant voices. I couldn't get the words, but they seemed to be arguing. Finally, I heard a couple of bolts draw back and the door opened.

A plump, matronly woman with steel-gray hair tied back in a bun confronted me just inside the door. There was no welcome in her look.

"Hello, Mrs. Wilson. Pleased to meet you."

"You're here about Dan?" Her voice was flat and cold as a frozen lake.

"Yes, ma'am. I've been hired by your lawyer, Mr. Louchs, to get to the bottom of this."

"Well there ain't no bottom to get to. Poor boy's been dead these past seven years."

"Perhaps we could sit down and discuss it for a minute?"

She turned on her heel and walked through a doorway to her left. I couldn't tell if she intended to lead me somewhere or if she was just walking away. I decided to follow and found myself in a small living room, spotlessly clean. It was a fussy, feminine room, done in soft peach, with lace trim on the sofa pillows and knickknacks on all the horizontal surfaces. I tried to keep my elbows tucked in.

Mrs. Wilson sat in a wing chair. Lisa was sitting on the sofa. "Mr. Garrett. How are you?" She stood up to shake hands. She was wearing a long black skirt and a white lace blouse. There was also a little bit of lipstick and a hint of eye makeup. She smiled at me, but her palm was moist and her movements were awkward. I had the sense that she was upset with her mother.

"Ma'am, I know this is difficult, but I need to talk to you about your son."

"No more difficult now than seven years ago," she said flatly. "He's dead, simple as that. Can't you understand that?"

"I'm sure it's clear enough in your mind, but we have to convince a judge. The only things he'll know about the case are the things that come out in court. Your lawyer has asked me to help him investigate.''

"You mean I'm paying you?" I'd worked some tough people before, but she was a peach.

"Indirectly, yes.''

"Then you might as well get on with it. If this is costing me money.''

I took a breath. "When did you last see Daniel?"

"The day he died.''

"And where was that?''

"Right here.''

"What time?''

"That morning. I don't remember exactly.''

"What were his plans?''

"He and Lisa were going shopping. Look, didn't you already ask her all this?''

I had to admit she was right. "Did he seem despondent or out of sorts around the time he disappeared?''

"No. And why do I have to keep telling you, he's dead.''

"What makes you say that?''

"His car was found empty, shot full of holes, and full of blood. Don't take a lawyer to figure that one out.''

"Do you have any other reason to think he's dead?''

She gave me a look normally reserved for morons and said nothing. "Look,'' I persisted. "Do you still have any of his things?''

"No. Threw them all away.''

"Do you have a recent picture?''

"Now how could I have that?'' she said sarcastically.

This woman was getting under my skin. "I mean, of course, from just before his—death."

"Nope."

I persisted. "Have you heard from him?"

"No."

"Are you in touch with any of his old friends?"

"No."

"Ma'am, I'm working for you, trying to help you—"

"Then get on with finding his body and leave me in peace! That's the only thing you can do that would be any good to me."

"I'm sorry. I know how this must hurt. Thank you for your time."

Lisa showed me to the door. "I'm sorry about Mom," she whispered. "She's never gotten over it. Dan was her only son, and he was the baby of the family."

"It must be hard."

"She's going to hurt anyway. Talking about it doesn't make it all that much worse. It may even help." She changed her tone. "You've had a busy day."

"I'm on a tight schedule and it's not over yet."

"Now where do you go?"

"I'm going to meet with Chief Ziemer again. Maybe look at the scene with him."

"But you were already there, weren't you?"

"I'm sorry about the added expense, but I need to do this case my way."

"No, not the money. Just why go back there again?"

"Because something very funny is going on. When I went there last night a car followed me.

They were from organized crime. After I met with you this morning they brought me in for a talk.''

"A talk? Why?''

"They seem to think I'm trying to find out who killed Dan.''

Her brow furrowed. "But you're in the case for a limited purpose, aren't you?''

"Yes. That's one of the things I had to explain to them.''

"Did they want you off the case!''

"Not after I talked to them. But that was the idea at first.''

"They threatened the last investigator, didn't they? That's why he dropped the case?''

I didn't know what Mark had told her. Knowing Mark, he had probably concocted something. "I don't know.''

She frowned at my answer, but didn't press it. "Why don't you drop it?''

"I'm in it. There's no time to give this to somebody else. I have to finish it.''

"What do you think you'll learn from the police?''

"I don't know. That's why I'm going.''

"Good luck.'' She smiled. "And sorry again about Mom.''

7

SATURDAY, 8:00 P.M.

After I left, I stopped at Lankenau Hospital. The days of a phone booth on every corner are gone, even downtown in major cities. Looking for a public phone that works is a crapshoot. But hospitals always have phones.

I reached Ziemer through the department radio paging system and told him I had some new information. He agreed to meet me at eight that night at the scene.

It was nearly six-thirty when I reached my apartment. No one seemed to be following. I looked around quickly and satisfied myself that the place hadn't been searched. After throwing a couple of pieces of pizza in the microwave, I changed into the clothes I'd worn the night before: jeans, a work shirt, and my parka. I was out the door again, the pizza on a paper plate, within ten minutes.

The turnpike unfolded under my lights as I rolled west. As I ate with one hand, I tried to make some sense of it all. Twenty-four hours before, I thought the possibilities were either a disappearance or a mob execution. Those were good starting points, and now the investigation was supposed to be narrowing. Having talked to everyone there was to talk to, except Brogan, I was no closer to eliminating either possibility. Now, I also had Ziemer's random killer theory to consider. And the possibility that it was a revenge killing by a disgruntled criminal client unconnected to the organization. The case was still moving in the wrong direction.

I hesitated, now that I had cleared things with Strasnick, to think that anyone was lying to me. I don't assume that everything that doesn't check out a hundred percent is a deliberate lie; more often than not, bad information is the result of innocent mistakes and assumptions. Besides, Strasnick had no motive to lie, at least no financial motive. And why shouldn't Mrs. Dosterburg tell the truth? She was even less affected by the outcome that Strasnick. Unless she had told me some half-truths to get me to come back again. . . .

The Morgantown exit came up. I was a couple of minutes ahead of schedule, and the pizza was sticking in my throat. I hit the drive-through at the McDonald's and ordered a large Coke. As I waited I started thinking about the past. My ex-wife and I had been here before. The first time she took the bar exam, right after she finished, we booked a room at the hotel next door or celebrate. After all, who ever really flunked the Pennsylvania bar exam? It was the middle of August; the weather was breezy and warm the whole weekend. We rode around the farm country in Amish buggies and went to Gettysburg. We ate bland Pennsylvania Dutch food in family-style restaurants with improbable names like Plain & Hearty and Amos' Country Cookin' that were really owned by Jews from New Jersey. And we fucked our brains out. She left her diaphragm at home and packed her most wicked black-lace negligee; she wanted to launch her career and our family at the same time.

I threw the empty cup out the window.

I drove up Route Ten past the scene, checking for a tail. Then I hunted around till I found the road that led up the bank on the west side of the highway. It was a small dirt road, partly overgrown. If the ground hadn't been frozen I would have been stuck for sure. It started on the right-hand side of Route Ten about a quarter of a mile north of the shooting. It climbed the bank in one steep swoop and then ended in the large flat area I'd been on the night before. No one was there, and in my headlights all I could find was the single set of tire tracks that led to the point where they had watched. I drove back down again and waited.

Eight-thirty had come and gone when the chief pulled up.

"Sorry to be late now. Had an accident to work over near Birdsboro."

"No problem, Chief. We get used to waiting in this business."

"So you solve this here case now?"

"Not exactly. No, not by a long shot. But I wanted to tell you what happened out here last night." I told him about the other car, leaving out the plate number and the fact that I had carried a gun. I also left out my conversation in Philadelphia that morning.

"Well, now," he said when I was through.

"It's a heck of a thing," I offered.

"Yeah. Ain't it, though?"

I looked down and kicked the dirt. In my experience, kicking the dirt is essential in dealing with the Pennsylvania Dutch. Long silences also help. And if the conversation is about buying something, squint in the sun and shove your hands in your back pockets.

"Well," he said at last. "What do you think now?"

"I think it was a Mafia thing. I don't know why the body disappeared, but I can't explain otherwise why they would be so interested."

"Well, that could be," he conceded.

"Tell me, what did you find out about the victim's background, as far as what kind of lawyer he was?"

"That wasn't my case, back then. If Dietz didn't check it out more thorough, then he didn't. We were both sergeants then, but he was senior. I tried to give him advice but he didn't want to listen. As a matter of fact, I told him he ought to call down to the district attorney in Philadelphia and ask around about this fella. He said he'd done it. Looks like he didn't."

"Would your getting to be chief have anything to do with his moving away?"

"That was his call. He was welcome to stay. Anyway, looks like he wasn't too careful back then."

"Yeah."

"Don't know where it would have led, though, anyway."

"No. Hard to say."

"You know, though. This does explain one thing."

"Oh?"

"The sister, Lisa. Now I expect family to be real upset when this stuff happens, but I get the feeling from talking to Dietz that she was worse than normal. Why, she was too scared to even get out of her car. She made him interview her in the car. Dietz didn't put that in. He said afterward that it made him look too much a softy. He felt real sorry for her. We all did."

"Did she say why?"

"Just scared, she said. I guess of the Mafia, now that I've heard what you said."

I nodded.

"And another thing."

"Yeah?" I asked.

"Talk to her mom?"

"Couple hours ago."

"Tough old bird, ain't she?"

"I've gotten more cooperation out of alligators."

"She was the same with us. Called us a bunch of fools for not catching the killers, but wouldn't help us an inch. Wouldn't even give us a recent picture. Said it wouldn't do any good anyway."

"Think she was scared, too?"

"That, or just contrary. Some folks are now."

I waited, but the chief had exhausted his store of information. "Tell me, Chief. Where is the car now?"

"Still around," he said vaguely.

"I'd like to take a look, if I may."

"If you don't mind doin' a little drivin', I suppose there's no harm. Just don't sit inside. The sta-teys say they're working on some new tests that might show something new.''

"Like what?"

"Couldn't say. I think they just want me to keep my nose out of the case. They figure they can solve it themselves.''

"So where is it?"

"You know the area round Blue Ball and Honey-brook?"

"Yeah."

"You know a Highway Three-Twenty-two?"

"Do I? I know Fetterville," I said, naming a collection of four houses and a light machine shop on 322 just east of Blue Ball.

"Well, now. You're all fixed up then. At the top of the hill, right before you get to the landfill, County Line Auto Salvage is on your right. That's where it is.''

"Do I need an appointment or permission?"

He shook his head. "It's open. No problem."

"Thanks. And like I said, if I find anything out I'll let you know.''

"Appreciate that."

"One more thing, Chief, while we're here. Can you help me place just where the car was found?"

"I didn't see it myself, but Dietz and I walked the site when there were still tire tracks from the Pinto and he showed me. Here, let me get my flashlight.''

He went back to his car and produced a flashlight half the size of a baseball bat. Ziemer was no small man, but I could see from the way he carried it that it was heavy. Until they were banned, the Philadelphia police carried flashlights like that. They were basically clubs that also happened to throw light.

Our cars were parked just off the road. He led me down the trail until we were at least twenty yards from the road and shone the light on the ground. "Right about here now."

I looked back. Route Ten was visible if you looked directly west, but thick trees pressed closed on both sides. "Pictures didn't show this well."

"I think the stateys towed it out to the road to take their pictures. Couldn't get good light on it back here. Trees were too close in on either side to set up the floodlights proper."

"Well, isn't that something," I said.

"What's that?"

"Lisa said she saw the car as she drove by on Ten."

"Remember that seven years ago those trees were thinner and lower. And there would have been fresh tire tracks leading off the road in the snow up to here."

"The side windows were shot out. Where was the glass?"

"From the driver's side, a lot of it stayed inside. But the passenger's window went outward, all over the place. There was a bunch on the main road a few yards south of the lane."

"So if the car had been going north, that's right where you would have expected to find it?"

"Oh, yeah."

"Do you know if the glass was visible?"

"I didn't see it, myself. But Dietz did. Said it

was real sparkly, real visible. That's how he was able to find the little lane here.''

Gritting my teeth, I started back for the main road. "Chief, can you answer a question for me?''

"Maybe.''

"Is there *any* evidence in this case that's inconsistent with *any* of the ideas about what happened?''

"Oh, no. That'd be too easy now, wouldn't it?''

I liked a man who could laugh at the world, especially when he was a cop.

We stood beside our cars. "So you headin' home now?'' he asked.

I spoke as casually as I could. "It's not too late yet. You know, what you told me about the sister's got me thinking. I think I might just stop by her place.'' I didn't tell him that she wouldn't be there.

8

SUNDAY, 2:00 A.M.

Lisa lived in the coal regions. It was sad, worn-out country, full of dead hopes, slag piles, rusted machinery, and innumerable hills that yielded vistas of nothing at all. The towns were half-empty, and the people that remained were mainly the old and those unwilling to take the inevitable beating on the resale of their houses. To the extent that the area still had an economy, it was largely fueled by money earned by men who lived in New Jersey or Philadelphia during the week, six or eight to a motel room, then came home on weekends to drink it away and beat up their wives and each other. I was glad it was dark; all I needed to consider was the dirty snow piled high on each side of the highway.

North Carbon, where Lisa lived, was in the heart of the region, a few miles north of Pottsville between two ridges. Some Philadelphians confuse Pottsville with Pottstown, a bustling and prosperous neo-suburb between Reading and Philadelphia. No one who has been in coal country would make that mistake.

The town's last real prosperity ended with the

Korean War. It looked neglected and tired; there
was nowhere to go but downhill, and the town knew
it. The shame of it was that it wasn't even fighting.
Even in the dark I could see that not one clapboard
house in ten had anything close to a decent coat of
paint. Except for a secondhand store and a couple
of real estate offices, the main business street was
one continuous abandoned storefront.

I was hungry, and the only thing open I could
see was an old hotel with a gravel parking lot full
of pickup trucks and motorcycles. A half-dozen
men in baseball caps and work boots were going
up the steps, and I decided to stop. I rolled down
my window and caught the heavy, pleasant smell
of frying hamburgers. Then they turned and looked
at me. I knew the look and what it meant; I started
the engine and kept moving.

Near the edge of town I found a convenience
store with gas pumps. The girl behind the counter,
who paid no attention to me, must have weighed
two hundred and fifty pounds. She had the oily skin
and flat hair of the morbidly obese. Her hands were
still pretty; I found myself wondering what she'd
be like without the weight.

"Got any hot dogs?"

"Just durin' the day," she said indifferently.

"Anything hot at all? It's sure cold outside."

"I shut off the stuff at five."

"Could you make me up a sandwich?"

She gestured vaguely around the shelves. "We
got lotsa candy bars." It was true enough. I picked
out two and a can of soda.

"Say, would you know a Lisa Wilson? She's supposed to live around here. Dark hair, middle thirties.''

She never looked up from the register. ''Nah. I don't pay much attention.'' She was starting to breathe hard from the extended conversation. I picked up my change and left. Back in my car I opened one of the candy bars, thought about the clerk, and wrapped it up again.

Lisa's questionnaire listed her address simply as ''two miles due west of North Carbon.'' It was all the identification that was necessary. Only one road, or at least only one paved road, answered that description, a potholed and washboarded mess that hadn't seen maintenance in years. The countryside around North Carbon was covered with about four inches of snow; past the edge of town there was no sign of plowing or sanding on the road. I picked my way carefully around the largest potholes. Once I had to go completely onto the shoulder to avoid a trench formed by a string of three large potholes that would have blocked a small tank from using the road. I began to appreciate the advantages of a pickup as my Honda bottomed out for the tenth time.

The road twisted and climbed, trying to escape the narrow river valley. There was no sign of life on either side except for occasional junked cars. Then, just as my odometer showed two miles, a light appeared on my right. It was a porch light for an old brick farmhouse, one story. The mailbox said WILSON in two-inch-high gold decals. I drove by slowly, taking my time. The house was facing the road, cut into the side of the hill, with the driveway on the right side. No garage. No fence. The house wasn't large, and the porch light was big enough to illuminate not only the front porch, but part of the front yard, too. No sign of a dog, at least not outside.

I kept going until I found the next house, which was a rusting trailer three-quarters of a mile further on. Half a dozen wrecked cars were scattered about in various stages of disassembly. The trailer was tilted about ten degrees to the left and was leaning so far toward the road that I thought it could topple over at any time. No lights were showing, and in most places I would have assumed it was abandoned junk. But when I used the driveway to turn around, I saw a dim light come on at the window.

I would have preferred to park my car away from her house, but there was simply no place any closer than town. Turning off my lights, I groped my way back down the hill until I could see the porch light up ahead on my left. Then I cut the engine and drifted closer. I rolled down the window and waited; there was no sound anywhere. Restarting the engine, I pulled into her driveway. Fortunately she had shoveled it out. There was even enough room for me to turn around and point the nose of the car back toward the road. I backed up as far as I could, nearly to the rear of the house.

What was I looking for? I didn't really know. If Ziemer was right, Dan was dead. If Strasnick was right, he was in hiding as far away as a lot of money would take him. I had no reason to disbelieve either of them. And even if I had, there was nothing to make me think he was in this little house in North Carbon in the middle of the night. But somehow I was convinced that Lisa wasn't telling me everything; that the move back east could have been to help Dan hide out, or to help him in some other way. Then again, my convictions weren't always the best guide. At various times in my life I'd been convinced that the Pennsylvania Supreme Court had a heart, that McGovern could beat Nixon, and that it would fall off if you played with it too much.

In the final analysis, I was there because I hadn't the slightest idea what else to do.

I climbed some steps to the back porch and found a door with a pane of glass in the top half. I shined in my pencil flashlight; it was the kitchen. The door was locked, but the bolt was cheap. A couple of minutes with my picks and the door was open. A real pro could have done it in twenty seconds. Closing and locking the door behind me, I went through the house.

The furniture, mostly dark wood Spanish pieces and a chrome-and-glass table, had nothing to do with the house. I suspected that Lisa had brought it back from Los Angeles. The broad-plank pine floors were bare except for a few pseudo-Navaho area rugs. Framed prints announcing LA art exhibits, some of them years ago, appeared on several walls. Above the tiny brick fireplace, now in use as an outlet for a wood stove, were matching framed pictures of Lisa and her mother.

The layout inside was very simple, just four rooms. The front half was divided into a living room and a bedroom; the rear half was two-thirds a kitchen and one-third a bathroom. There was no upstairs or basement. The stove was out, but the house was still quite a bit warmer than outside. I took off my parka and threw it over one of the chairs.

Starting in the bedroom, I went to work. In the corner was a small desk with four drawers. Not that it made much difference, but they were unlocked.

Whenever I go into a house looking for documents, I think of all the times, as a lawyer, I had to obtain duplicate insurance policies, certificates of divorce, deeds, and car titles for clients who had misplaced them in their own homes and couldn't find them again, even with all the time in the world. But in the movies, the detective goes into a strange house, immediately goes to the correct floor, room, and piece of furniture, opens the correct drawer, looks briefly at one or two pieces of paper, and then finds what he needs. Crap.

Being right-handed, and there being no better place to start, I pulled open the lower right-hand drawer. It contained some current ledgers and account books from a company called Pottsville Fabricating. The upper right-hand drawer was her liquor cabinet: two bottles of white wine, a bottle of gin, and a six-pack of small bottles of tonic water. Next, in the lower left-hand drawer, I found her personal papers. The bills were the routine things: utilities, car repairs, car insurance, and a small MasterCard account balance. I went over the phone bills carefully. She had saved them for the last year, and the only out-of-the-area calls were to Philadelphia. The number matched her mother's phone. The other listed calls were almost all to Pottsville Fabricating. No address book, at least that I could find. No letters saved from anyone. Her tax records for the last three years. Insurance papers for her car and medical insurance. Her canceled checks; except for some magazine subscriptions and a few small checks to people I couldn't identify, the checks that didn't match up with the bills were mostly to the Pottsville supermarket. Last, her bank statements, showing her biweekly salary as her only deposits during the last year. No mystery about where her money was going or where it was coming from.

The upper left-hand drawer seemed to be storage. The top item, in a black imitation-leather presentation case, was her nursing diploma from a Los Angeles hospital. Tucked into a corner was a snapshot, yellowed and creased, showing her in a nurse's uniform standing in front of a palm tree—a graduation shot, I guessed. It was overexposed and her face was in shadow, but it was definitely her. Next was her high school diploma. At the bottom was her passport, issued four years ago. The photograph showed Lisa deeply tanned, her hair pulled back, and smiling. The only stamping indicated a trip to Mexico shortly after it was issued.

The dresser was a cherry lowboy with six drawers and a large mirror. Except for a vibrator under her lingerie and an unopened box of condoms, I found nothing but her clothing.

The bathroom medicine cabinet was small and crammed with lipstick, makeup, cleaning solution for contact lenses, cold remedies, and the like. No tampons. A small bottle of generic aspirin and a half-used carton of generic antihistamines. One toothbrush. The only razor I could find was a woman's model solely for removing leg hair. No evidence that someone else lived here or even visited here.

I was thinking about whether I should bother to search the kitchen when I felt a draft on my neck. Had I left the back door open? Before I could turn around, something exploded in the back of my head. For an instant I was in searing pain as I fell forward. I barely remember my head slamming into the sink.

At first I was aware of a roaring in my ears. Was I at the beach? I couldn't tell; I seemed to be floating, but it was cold. And when I tried to move my arms, nothing happened. Still, the feeling of floating persisted. Then gradually, I don't know how long it took, the roaring faded. Through a red haze I saw a couple of dark objects. After a while I recognized them as my boots. I tried to move them and couldn't. Then I noticed that they weren't just brown; they were spattered with red. About that time I started to feel the pain.

"Hey, Red, I think he's coming around."

"No shit."

Even when I kept still the back of my head throbbed. When I tried to turn I felt I was going to pass out. I had a deep burning sensation all the way across my forehead. The taste of blood was strong in my mouth, and either my lip or my tongue was bleeding freely. The right side of my chest ached, and a knifelike pain ran across to the center of my chest if I took more than a very shallow breath. It was hard to breathe any deeper, anyway; my stomach ached. Repeated blows to the solar plexus, I thought.

The lights were all on. Two men. Not the two

from this morning. Bikers. Late twenties. Red was heavyset with a black tangled beard and heavily tattooed forearms. The other was tall and balding, with a Fu Manchu mustache. He wore a chain around his waist and carried a big hunting knife in his belt loop. Both wore black Harley-Davidson T-shirts. They both looked mean as hell. Not just bikers. Pagans.

I was in the kitchen in a chair, facing generally toward the rear window. My hands were tied behind me and my feet were tied to the chair. Gritting my teeth against the pain I looked down; flecks of blood were all around me. They'd tied me up and worked me over while I was out.

Red stood in front of me. Very deliberately, seeking the best footing, he took a stance with his feet wide apart. When he was satisfied, he put on a leather studded glove. Seeing it made me forget what I'd been through so far; one good swipe with that thing would take half my face off. The silver studs glinted in the light. He looked at me in satisfaction and pounded the glove into his palm. "Ready for some more fun, asshole?"

I opened my mouth to speak and found myself just spitting blood.

"Jesus, Red, ease up," the other called.

"Fuck off!"

"Fuck you! You screw up this job and you're in shit. You off him before he talks, you're gonna answer for it, not me, asshole."

"You need your fuckin' ass wiped."

"I don't need any trouble with the law. We got no protection if we don't follow orders. And if my parole gets violated I'm back in Huntington. You, too.''

"Let's do him the way we did that cunt who was hitchin'.''

"That doesn't get out of him what we need to know, fuckhead.''

"Okay, you're so goddam smart, what do we do?''

"Let him come around. Think about it a little. Then if he doesn't talk we use the propane torch on him.''

"No shit?''

"Terry and Joe did that last year to the snitch on the LSD bust. Stripped him and nailed him to his kitchen floor. Started on the soles of his feet and worked their way up to his eyes. They saved his balls for last. Took him all night to die.''

Red nodded and grunted. Reluctantly he took off the glove, though he couldn't resist kicking me in the shin as he walked past. The pain tore right up my leg to my hip. For a second I thought he'd broken my leg. I was nauseous, whether from fear or pain I couldn't tell. My only thought was that I didn't want to die that way.

The bleeding in my mouth was slowing down, and I was able to feel around with my tongue. I'd bitten into my lower lip, possibly when falling. Or when I was hit afterward. My hands and feet were securely tied; they had probably done this kind of thing before, who knows how many times. All I could do was turn my head, slowly, and try to think of a plan.

The house was a shambles. They were searching for something—as I was. Unlike me, they didn't care who knew about it. Every stuffed piece of furniture had been slashed open, every poster torn down, every drawer turned upside down and dumped on the floor. They made crackling noises as they walked from room to room, trampling everything underfoot.

I became aware of another type of crackling sound, higher in pitch and sharper. Tapping on glass. There, at the rear window, was Lisa.

Not daring to turn my head sharply, I looked around. Red was in the bedroom, tearing drawers out of the dresser. The other was in the living room. I looked back at her. She was holding up one finger and her eyebrows were raised in inquiry.

Ever so slightly, I shook my head no.

Two fingers.

Yes.

With the two fingers spread in a V, she pointed to the right, toward the bedroom. I shook my head no.

One finger pointed to the bedroom. Yes.

One finger straight ahead, toward the living room. Yes.

She pointed with two fingers, once at the bedroom and once at the living room. I nodded. Then she brought up her other hand and showed me a revolver. It looked barely bigger than a toy, but it looked a lot better than a propane torch. She stepped back slightly from the window; we settled down to wait.

It wasn't long. From the bedroom, Red yelled, "Hey, come and see this!" I don't know what caught his attention, but the other ambled in. I looked at the window and nodded. No danger of being surrounded now, they were both in the same place.

The rear door opened and she crept into the kitchen soundlessly, wearing the same jacket and jeans I'd seen that morning. Up close, the gun looked like a .22. A bazooka would have been my own choice for taking on these charmers. I was surprised she could move so quietly on the linoleum until I looked at her feet; she was only wearing her socks, and they were soaked through. I wondered how long she'd stood there in the snow.

She was about five feet to my right, holding the gun in front of her with both hands, when the two of them came out of the bedroom together. They were laughing about whatever they had found. They saw Lisa and the gun and their laughter stopped.

"Hold it right there and put your hands up." I cringed; it was all wrong. Her voice was nervous and diffident. And she was holding the gun wrong— both hands wrapped around the grip, fully extended. She was halfway to handing him the gun already.

Red was an old hand at intimidation. "Well, little lady, suppose you hand that over to me." He smiled and took a step forward.

She took a step back. "Stop right there."

He smiled more broadly and took another step. "Now you're not gonna shoot no one lady. Just hand over that thing before someone get hurt."

She shook her head.

"Come on now, baby." He was taking slow steps, but big ones, and he was right in front of me. No more than four feet from her. And his hand was reaching out. It was almost on the gun.

At that moment the world exploded. A thunderclap of sound and a flash of light leapt from the gun, and a neat black hole appeared in the palm of Red's hand. For an instant his arm seemed to deform and waver; I realized that the bullet had tunneled right through his wrist and up his forearm.

As he bent over, clutching his arm, the other one made his move. His knife was ready. He must have eased it out while Red was going for the gun. Crouching down, he shoved Red to one side and charged. He knew his stuff. He kept the knife low, not far above his knees but the point high. He moved toward Lisa, aiming for her stomach.

Again an explosion almost in my right ear. The round went wild; I heard the tinkling of glass somewhere. Then she fired again, hitting him in the shoulder blade. He staggered back for a moment but came on again, the knife point almost touching her. But she never stepped back. She fired again; this time she caught him at the corner of his chin, laying his whole jaw open. Blood spurted everywhere and he went down. The knife clattered on the linoleum.

She moved the gun back to Red but the fight was out of him. Judging from the blood, she'd hit an artery in his wrist. He was pinching the wound shut with his good hand.

"Both of you, lie down on the floor in the living room." Red helped his friend to comply. There was no argument.

With one eye and the gun on them, she cut me loose. If there was pain when my circulation was restored, I didn't notice. She motioned to hand me the gun but I shook my head; I was in no shape to take charge. She nodded, but raised her eyebrows.

"Water," I managed to croak.

She brought me a large glass. I sipped, rinsed out my mouth, and spit on the floor. The shape the place was in, it didn't matter much anymore. Most of what came out was blood. I sipped some more and spit it out; still lots of blood, but more water this time. I kept going until it was basically water with just a trace of blood. Then I poured the rest over my head. Diluted blood ran everywhere; my face must have been covered with it.

I cleared my throat. If I kept my voice low and spoke slowly, I could talk.

"Listen up, assholes. Any good reason why we shouldn't blow your fucking heads off and say we caught you burglarizing the place? Which is true, by the way."

No response.

"Better give us a reason. Tell me who sent you."

Silence. I nodded to her.

Lisa walked over to Red, keeping the gun pointed in his face. "This is my house you wrecked. Tell me who you did it for."

Red looked up at her. "You ain't gonna shoot a man in cold blood, lady."

There were three very surprised people in the room when she lowered the gun and very deliberately shot him in the foot. When the echo died away—even a .22 makes a huge noise in a confined space—she raised the gun again. This time she pointed it at his groin. Their eyes met; I wondered what Red was seeing in her face.

"Who?" she asked quietly.

No response.

She cocked the gun and started squeezing the trigger.

He swallowed. "Guy with the mob in Philly. Don't know his name. We do jobs for them, muscle stuff, sometimes. He called and said to search the place and put the squeeze on anybody who was here."

She looked back at me, not moving the gun. I nodded. It was my turn.

"What else?" I asked. My mouth was bleeding again.

"Get rid of them afterward. But to get the information first."

"What information?"

"Where the stuff was."

"What's his name?"

"Don't know his name. Never did. No bullshit. He doesn't know mine either. We keep it that way. All I have is a P.O. box for him."

"What were you looking for?"

"A hundred grand in cash. Fifty-fifty split if we found it."

"How do you know he's mob?"

"He's in tight with them. He's one of their lawyers."

"You sure he's a lawyer?"

"Yeah and he said he had suck with all kinds of people if we got picked up. So long as we did like we were told we didn't have to worry about the law."

My vision was starting to go, and the room was moving away. They might know something more, but having them around if I passed out was an invitation to trouble. It was time to get rid of them. "Very slowly, take out your wallets and toss them over." I looked. I was not surprised to find nearly nine hundred dollars in one wallet and six hundred in the other. People like them had no credit and no bank accounts; and no legal explanation for the money they had. It was simpler to just carry it around with them.

"We'll consider this as compensation for the damages. Or we can all go see the police, if you're in the mood for a fall. I didn't think so. And we keep the ID. And toss me the car keys. That's good." I had to stop again to swallow. "Don't even think about payback. If anything ever happens out here, if so much as a squirrel farts, this goes to the DA and the state parole board. Now get out."

They struggled to their feet. Lisa stayed clear of them and kept the gun trained.

"Hey, man," Red pleaded at the door, "you can't make us walk to town like this. Without our coats. It's two fuckin' miles. And it's cold. We could *die* out there."

Slowly and painfully I stood up. The room spun around me. With my hand on the wall for balance I moved over until we were face-to-face. "I hope you do."

I don't actually remember them going out, but I recall hearing the door shut and their steps receding down the driveway. After that I must have passed out.

9

SUNDAY, 10:00 A.M.

It was the headache that woke me. When I opened my eyes it was light, but it took a while to orient myself. I was lying down. In her bedroom. On the bed, with the covers over me. It was warm and I could smell the close, pine scent of the wood smoke. The sun was well above the horizon. The windup alarm clock by the bed said 3:30 and its face was cracked. I wondered what they thought could possibly have been hidden in the clock.

I turned my head slightly to the left, trying to minimize my movements. The pain in my head and ribs was bad enough just lying still. Something dark was lying on the pillow next to me. I started to reach for it with my left arm and found it blocked; something was lying across my chest. I felt around; it was an arm. I followed it across my chest, from right to left, and found that it ended in a shoulder pressed against my left side. I moved further and touched a breast. The arm stirred and squeezed me gently; then the dark thing moved—it was Lisa's hair—and her sleepy face appeared. "How are you feeling?"

I moistened my lips. I tried to speak twice before I could get the word out. "Headache."

She got out of bed and for a moment I had a view of her back—tanned and freckled, and muscular. I was counting her ribs when she slipped on a bulky white robe. I heard the water running, and then she returned with a bottle of aspirin and a glass of water. Lisa and the aspirin looked equally good to me just then.

"Take four as a start," she said. "If that doesn't help take two more every half hour. Take them till either the pain goes away or your ears start to ring. Or until you shit black; that means your stomach lining is bleeding."

The aspirin would take a while to work, but the water at least lubricated my throat. I struggled to sit up and found that I was naked except for some tape on my ribs. The knifelike pain of last evening returned when I moved too quickly. With her help I managed to sit up and get some pillows behind me. When I was settled she sat next to me.

"How are you feeling?" she asked.

"It's time to talk. You go first. What you did last night."

"You ought to rest."

"Talk."

"Okay. Hanging around Mom's was getting on my nerves. Plus, we have to get our records at work to the accountant in the next few days. I decided to come home and work on the books today. I'm going away to Cancun for a long vacation when this mess is over, so I needed to get this done." She brushed her tousled hair away from her face. "I drove up and saw a pickup truck in the driveway. I pulled in and didn't see anyone. Then I saw your car. They had parked the pickup sideways so you were parked in. That's when I started to get scared. I remembered what you said about being warned off. I tiptoed around the back and saw you tied up. I went back to my car and got the gun.'' She saw my puzzled look. ''It's just an old twenty-two that I got on a trade when I moved up here. I have to shoot snakes in the woodpile every now and then. I haven't shot it in a couple of years.''

''You did fine.''

''It's a good thing a gun works no matter how scared you are. And it's a good thing the guy with the beard decided to talk. When I shot him in the foot that was my last bullet.''

I had an image of Red, his blood up from being shot twice, finding out we were defenseless. There must be a God, and he does love idiots. ''Oh.''

''After they left you passed out. I got your clothes off and cleaned you up. You're lucky; nothing that needs a doctor. It looks worse than it is. You have a big cut on the forehead, a cut in the inside of your lower lip, some bruises, tenderness in the back of your head. Nothing that needs stitches. And some bruised ribs. But''—she smiled—''You already knew about those.'' She picked up my left wrist, placed her thumb against my pulse, and looked at her wristwatch for a few seconds. ''Your pulse is good.''

''Where are my clothes?''

''There's no washing machine here. I mostly use the laundromat in town. But I rinsed them out in the sink and hung them near the stove. They'll be dry soon.''

"Good. Then we can go." I started to get up and was brought up short by the pain from my ribs.

"Easy there. You shouldn't be going anywhere. You need some rest."

"I've got a case. The hearing's tomorrow."

"You've got yourself half killed over it. Isn't that enough? Let it go."

"This is bigger than your brother. It's the mob and money and maybe drugs and who all knows what else. Whatever it is, it's big."

Before she turned her face away, I could see that it was flushed. "Just let it *alone*, will you? It was sheer luck you weren't killed. You've learned a lot, more than enough to make the judge happy. It's not worth it."

"I'm going ahead."

"None of this will bring Danny back."

I took my time speaking. My headache was worse, and the room was starting to spin. "Either I'm crawling out the door naked on my hands and knees, or I can do this with your help."

"I'm worried about you."

"I'm safer with you to help."

She turned back to me. "Okay, you idiot. I'll help. If you promise to stay in bed till noon, I'll drive you wherever you want."

"You didn't ask me what I was doing here."

"I thought you must have decided you needed to ask me some more questions, and you found out I'd left Mom's."

"No. I wanted to search your house when you weren't here."

Her eyes widened. "To see if Danny was *here*?"

"Yes. Or a lead to where he was. Or whether he's alive."

"Then—you didn't believe me."

"It's my job not to take things on faith."

"You mean, you thought he was hiding out with me? That I've been hiding him here all these years?"

I had to admit it sounded pretty stupid. "Maybe. I didn't know."

"It's like Mom said. You're looking in the wrong place. Go to the swamps in south Jersey, or wherever they hide the bodies."

We hadn't talked more than a couple minutes, but I was tired already. Black spots started moving in front of my eyes. I nodded yes and closed my eyes. I'm not sure if she had time to get off the bed before I went back to sleep.

When I woke up again, I smelled coffee and bacon. She came into the room wearing a sweatshirt and jeans, her hair pulled back, dragging a large plastic garbage bag behind her. My headache was only a little better; I took two more aspirin.

"You might as well take four. It's nearly noon."

"Is breakfast ready? Smells good."

"Been ready for an hour. Hey, hold it. Let me help you up."

By holding only my left arm, she was able to help me sit up without increasing the pain in my ribs. But standing brought on a wave of dizziness. The room spun around and started to go dark for a moment, and my knees buckled. She dug her hip into mine, judo-style, and supported me with her own legs. The moment passed and I was able to stand alone, with my left arm against the wall for balance. She helped me into her terry-cloth bath-robe and followed close behind as I worked my way along the wall into the kitchen.

I ate slowly, afraid of not keeping the food down. I looked around. Most of the wreckage had already disappeared, and the floor and walls were mopped clean of blood. The main reminders of the previous night were the ripped cushions and the bullet hole in one of the panes of the kitchen window.

"Lisa, will the money cover the damage?"

"No problem. It's funny how that doesn't seem important when you're just trying to stay alive. But the furniture didn't go with the place, anyway. It was just left over from my last apartment. It looked a lot better in LA than back here. How's your head?"

"Still hurts. But I feel better with some food in me. Could you get me my clothes and the aspirin?"

Supporting myself against the kitchen table, I stood up while she helped me off with the bathrobe and then helped me dress. Even though I was as sore and dizzy as ever, I felt better in my clothes. They were rumpled, torn, not fully dry, and still bloodstained in places, but at least I was dressed.

"Are you going to lie down again, I hope?" she asked.

"No; it's nearly one. We have a long day ahead of us."

"Why?" She crossed her arms over her chest and glared at me.

"Because I have a job to do."

"A job? You know what your job is? To get on the stand and say that nobody's heard from him in seven years. Period. End of story. That's all you have to say to meet the burden of proof. Now drop it."

"Somebody thinks there's more to this case than a disappearance, and they're going to a lot of trouble to find out."

"Well, they're right. Dan's dead, been dead this whole time. It's just that there's no body. Everyone can see that. And besides, you're hurt."

"Like I said, you can drive me or I'll do it myself."

"You are the most goddam frustrating stubborn man!"

"Help me up. I need to pee."

In the bathroom mirror, I studied my face. A gash clear across the forehead. Eyes sunken and bloodshot. The entire left side was red and puffy. And everything would probably look worse tomorrow. Still, my nose wasn't broken and none of the cuts were very deep. I thought of what I would have looked like after a session with the propane torch.

Between the food and the aspirin, the headache was a little better. The dizziness was another matter. Every change of position sent things spinning. As casually as possible I worked my way along the wall back to the kitchen and sat down.

"Lisa, come sit with me a minute. We have to talk." I realized how much I disliked doing this, which made me angry with myself. So what if she'd saved my life? Business was business and I had a job. I had no right either liking or disliking it.

Still angry, she sat across the table from me. Before I started I took two more aspirin with the last of the coffee. I could feel a new headache coming on, this one in the front of my head.

"The night Dan disappeared, what time did you finish shopping?"

"I don't remember."

"Try again."

"It's been a long time. Can you remember what time you finished watching TV seven years ago?"

"You were at the Park City Mall in Lancaster, right?"

She nodded slightly. She knew enough to be suspicious when people asked questions to which they already knew the answer.

"And your dinner reservation was for what time?"

"I don't remember. Nine. Or later maybe. He made it, anyway."

"The restaurant says it was for eight."

"If that's what they say."

"It's an hour's drive from Park City to Morgantown."

"So? I mean, I think that's right."

"The police checked the purchase slips in your car."

"They prove I was shopping at Park City that day."

"Yes, and then some. Did you know that some of the slips have the time, not just the date?"

"I don't know."

I took a leap. "Lisa, if I told you that Park City wasn't even open that late on Sunday nights, would that help you remember?"

Silence.

Another leap. "If I told you that none of your purchases were after five?"

"I don't know; then I must have left earlier."

"Like five?"

"Maybe. I don't remember."

"And what did you do then?"

She weighed each word carefully. "Drove around

and looked at other stores that were still open. Drove through the Amish country and watched the buggies going home after church services. Lancaster County is all farms and hills. Even in the middle of winter it's prettier than the countryside around LA. I was just killing time till dinner. But so what?''

"There was an awful lot of time to kill between five and eight. There isn't a hell of a lot going on in Lancaster County on a Sunday night in the wintertime." It was time to press my luck. "At a restaurant that fancy, most customers arrive early and have a drink at the bar while they wait for their tables.''

"I wouldn't know what Dan had planned. He'd been there before, not me.''

"So you would have wanted to arrive at seven, seven-thirty.''

"I told you, I don't know.''

"But the time all fits. You leave Park City at five, drive around for maybe an hour, plan to arrive around seven. You wanted to stretch a one-hour drive into two hours at the most. No more.''

"So?''

"It proved you did something for the better part of three hours you never told the police about." Or me, either, but I didn't say that.

"Now hold on a minute. Even if I left Lancaster at five, if we were going to meet for a drink at seven, that would only leave one hour unaccounted for—and I just told you what I did. Drove around.''

"No. I mean what you did *after* the shooting.''

Her face froze. I let the silence stretch out for a good thirty seconds. She must have been breathing but I couldn't see her chest moving.

"Lisa, you called in the shooting at ten-thirty.

You never told the police exactly what time you found the car, but you gave the impression that it was around ten, or even a little after. But the shooting happened at seven, not ten, right?''

''Wait a minute. How can I possibly know when that happened?''

''Because you were there.''

''I told you—''

''I know what you told me. And what you told the police. And it doesn't make sense. If he was coming up from Philadelphia, he would have used the turnpike and taken the Morgantown exit. You say he was supposed to meet you right there. Why would he drive right past your meeting place and go up Route Ten by himself for half a mile?''

''I have no way of knowing why. Maybe he wasn't coming from Philly. He could have been seeing a client somewhere else. West Chester or somewhere.''

Time to try another tack, even if it wasn't based in fact. ''And how did you spot the car? It was back in the woods so far it couldn't be seen from the road.''

''Of course it could be seen. You say you saw the police photographs.''

Sometimes a lie gets you to the truth. ''With headlights shining on it, of course you could see it. But if you were driving by, your headlights wouldn't have picked it up. It was too far off the road and hidden in the trees.''

''I told you, I saw it. That's that.''

She didn't mention the glass particles in the roadway. If she'd found the car the way she said, she'd have to know about them. I took the biggest leap of all. "Lisa, you had to have been in the car. The person who was shot was the passenger, not the driver."

"What are you talking about?"

"The spatter marks from the blood prove it. And the car was moving when the shots were fired, so there had to be a driver. Plus, after somebody was shot in that car, someone was able to turn into that little side lane and get it stopped. Someone who was in good enough control to stop without hitting the trees on either side. Nobody shot with a forty-five at close range is going to be driving that carefully." She shook her head but I paid no attention. "And if the driver wasn't hit, the passenger was. There was never a second car, was there? You were both in the same car, and you were driving."

"Why are you doing this?"

"Because Monday afternoon I have to swear to what I think happened. And I'm not going to help prove a case that he's dead if I think that the key witness isn't giving it to me straight."

Her face was still stone, but at least she was breathing again.

I softened my voice. My headache was worse, and the room was starting to wobble even though I was still sitting down. "Lisa, you may not think so right now, but I'm on your side. You saved my life and I'm grateful. But we need to be able to trust each other. Come on now, come clean."

She took a deep breath and looked down at her hands. I waited.

"Is what I say confidential?"

I had to think for a moment. She was entitled to the right answer, not just the convenient one. "Yes.

I've been hired by an attorney and I'm working under his direction. So the attorney-client privilege
applies.''

"There was only one car. We were together. We
left from Mom's place late that morning, went to
Reading, then to Lancaster. We left the mall around
five, drove around the Amish country like I said. I
was driving because Dan was tired. Then we drove
to Morgantown and started north on Ten. It was a
little after seven.''

I nodded and swallowed two aspirin dry. "Go˙
on.''

"It was dark, of course. A car came up behind
us and started to pass. I remember thinking that
they must either know the road well or be in a big
hurry, because the road was so full of curves. Then
as it pulled alongside us I heard a backfire, real
close, and then another. I looked over. There was
a passenger in the other car; his window was down
and he was pointing something at us. I didn't see
what it was, but then I knew it had to be a gun. I
couldn't tell anything about him except that it was
a man. I yelled 'Duck' and tried to keep my own
head down. Then there was a huge crash and my
side window exploded. Glass was everywhere—in
my hair, all over the place. I jammed on the brakes.
There were some more shots, I don't know how
many. Just as I was getting the car to a stop I saw
the lane and pulled in. The other car slowed down
but then a couple of other cars came up from Morgantown and it speeded up. It went out of sight
behind a bend not far away. I got the car into the
lane and out of sight.''

"It was only then you had time to look at Dan?''

She nodded. "He must not have had time to duck. There was—there was a hole in the middle of his forehead. He must have been looking toward the other car. His eyes were still open; he just looked surprised. By the time I got the car stopped and looked at him, the bleeding was already slowing down. I knew then that he'd died instantly."

"And what happened next?"

"For a minute, nothing. I was hysterical. Then I realized that they might be coming back for me. They must have seen that there were two people in the car, and they couldn't be sure they'd taken care of both. And I knew they weren't far away. There was nothing I could do for Dan. If there had been, I would have stayed. Or carried him, or whatever had to be done. But there wasn't. So I got out of the car and walked to the road. I walked back to Morgantown. Whenever a car came by I moved over into the bushes. Then when I got back to a phone, I called Mom and told her what had happened."

"She drove up and gave you her car."

"Right. While she was on her way up I thought of a plan. It took her the better part of an hour and a half to get there, maybe longer, so I had time to think. I decided to tell the police that I hadn't been at the scene. I knew that would get into the newspapers. When they—those people—read that I hadn't seen anything, I thought they might leave me alone."

"But what if they saw you in the car? You were closer to them, you were driving."

"Even so, it was my way of telling them I wasn't going to say anything."

"Okay. So you left your mom in Morgantown because you couldn't afford to have her seen."

"Right. At the McDonald's. So I went back to the car. I was just going to get out my packages and put them in Mom's car. In the backseat. After all, I couldn't have explained how my stuff was in his car if we hadn't been together. But when I got there he was gone."

"Any footprints?"

Just on the driver's side; nothing on his side. And I'd gotten out the driver's side myself. From the blood it looked like he'd been taken out the driver's side. Finding him gone scared me even more. They knew where the car was and they'd been back. For all I knew they were watching me right then. So I got my packages and got out of there as quick as I could."

"Then you stopped somewhere, washed up, combed the glass out of your hair, and called the police."

"Right. And you know the rest. And now you know why I'm so sure he's dead."

"I wish you'd told me this before."

"I have to stay with what I told the police. Even now. What if they find out that I was an eyewitness?"

"I have to share this with your attorney. But I think we can win without having to disclose any of this in open court."

"We have to. I'm sticking to my original story at the hearing. I'd rather drop the case or perjure myself than give them a reason to come after me after all this time."

"I'll make that clear to Mark." I was basically through with my questions, but I wanted to ease out of it slowly. Our nerves were both raw and I couldn't leave things like this. "Now what did Dan really tell you about his involvement with Mafia cases?"

"He never used that word. He was ashamed of that work. But sometimes when he'd talk about a drug or extortion or bribery case, you had the feeling that it was part of a bigger operation."

"Did he ever mention names or particular clients?"

"Oh, no. I don't think he was allowed to, anyway."

"Why would they have wanted him dead?"

"I don't know."

"Did he ever say anything to you to suggest that he was concerned for his safety?"

"No. That last couple of days we were together he seemed a little edgy, like something from the office was bothering him, but he didn't say anything in particular. It didn't seem that big a deal, either; more like there was some misunderstanding with a client or someone that had to be worked out. But I'm sure he would have told me if he thought he was in danger."

I had managed to get a good hundred yards further up the same blind alley. At least the aspirin were finally helping. Also, I was able to get up unassisted, as long as I braced myself on the back of the chair. "Let's go."

"How do you feel?"

"Fit as a goddam fiddle."

"I doubt that."

"We're going."

"Okay."

10

SUNDAY, 1:00 P.M.

Gingerly I maneuvered my right arm into my parka while Lisa held out the sleeve. It was painful enough to convince me not to try to take it off unless absolutely necessary, but at least the ribs stayed where they should, outside my lungs.

When we stepped outside, the afternoon was cloudless and cold. The tops of the pines were swaying, but in their shelter all we felt was a slight breeze. The drive in front of my car was empty except for Lisa's car and a complex of tire tracks; the Pagans must have come back with a second set of keys while we were asleep. I was glad to see it gone. We had no use for it—and anyway, it showed me they were still alive. Last night I wanted them dead, but not now.

My first thought was to take my own car, but then I thought again. The boys in Philly knew the car. Lisa's might get past them.

My dizziness refused to go away, but I discovered that I could walk around unassisted as long as I took each step deliberately, like a drunk trying to walk without a stagger. I went to my car, got out the .357 magnum, and checked to make sure it was still loaded. It was. Then I turned one of the pockets of my parka inside out and tore a one-inch hole in the lining. When I replaced the pocket and put the gun in it, the barrel went through the hole, and the rest of the gun fit comfortably in the pocket. I got out my camera, loaded it with 100 ASA, and locked up the car again.

I got in Lisa's car, a five-year-old brown sedan with one green door and more than its share of body rust. She had seen the revolver. "Where did that come from?"

"I keep it under the seat."

"What for?"

"Protection against being ambushed or forced off the road or confronted while stuck inside the car. I've been lucky; I've never needed it."

"Why such a big gun?"

"A thirty-eight special or even a nine millimeter won't reliably penetrate a car door. If it hits just sheet metal it'll go through, but a piece of bracing or the door-latch mechanism will stop it. If I'm ever in enough trouble to have to use a gun, I don't intend to show it first."

I had to close the door with my left hand, and finding a comfortable position was hard. I had to settle for a peculiar contortion that left me leaning heavily to the left and half twisted toward the driver.

"Where to?" she asked.

"We're headed for a junkyard near Honeybrook, Chester County. For the moment, head for Reading. Take Route Sixty-one."

She pulled out and started down the hill toward town.

"What's the plan?"

"The car is in a junkyard, impounded by the police as evidence. I want to give it a look. And there's a friend of Daniel's I want to talk to."

"Why?"

"As for the car, I want to see it for myself. And take a few pictures. I can run them through a one-hour photo service on Monday and have some pictures for the lawyer to show the judge. Let him see for himself what we're talking about."

"Didn't the police take photos?"

"I told them I'd leave them out of it if I could. They gave me a lot of cooperation. Plus, if we subpoenaed the chief, there's no telling what he might say. Especially if the insurance company's lawyers got lucky on cross."

"I don't understand."

"I don't know if he'd really do this, but suppose he starts rambling about how the case is full of loose ends and unanswered questions and how peculiar it is because they've always solved their homicides before? It starts raising doubts in the judge's mind about this disappearance."

"But it's not a disappearance."

"But you're not going to be testifying."

"Don't they have to call me to explain what happened?"

"You mean, so you can say what you said to the police?"

"Yes."

"That would be perjury."

She was silent until we turned right at the town's

red light and onto the main highway. "Yeah, you're right. I've been living with what I told them so long that it doesn't occur to me to tell the truth anymore, even when I should."

"It's up to Mark, but I figure I'll testify about the car and the disappearance. Keep you out of it."

"But you weren't there. Isn't that hearsay or something?"

"Not if Mark qualifies me as an expert criminologist. Then I can give my expert opinion about whether there was a homicide and base it upon hearsay I've received from others."

"Will they let you do that?"

"In Pennsylvania, in a civil case, with no jury, almost certainly."

"So you need to see the car firsthand?"

"Yeah. But you don't have to see it."

"It's just a car, now."

We drove for a few miles in silence. My headache returned, and I swallowed some more aspirin.

"There's something I should tell you," she said. "About my coming home last night."

"I'm glad you did. I haven't really thanked you."

"Oh, I'm sure you will. But what I wanted to tell you was, I came home last night to see if you would be looking around."

I hadn't quite accepted her story, but I was still surprised. "What happened to make you think I'd go to your place?"

"Nothing in particular. Just that Mom was so difficult and there was so little time—and I could see how badly you wanted to get to the bottom of the case. It was just a feeling."

"Thanks for telling me."

"You know, I never imagined going through anything like last night. It's really true that you can be too scared to do anything, even if it means saving your own life."

"It must have brought back some memories for you."

"With Danny it was all over in a moment. This was something that I had to gear myself up to do. Want to know something? Even if you hadn't signaled they were both in one end of the house, I was going to come in anyway. I was afraid I'd lose my nerve if I waited any longer."

"Or freeze your feet off."

"I never felt a thing. Not numb, I mean; I just never noticed."

"You did fine."

"Once I fired the first shot, you mean. From then on it was rolling. Getting started was the hard part."

"You sure surprised Red, there at the end, shooting him in the foot."

"He made it easy. When he wanted the gun away from me, at first, he was so nice, asking me to do him a favor. And I knew it was bullshit, but I almost did it anyway. But later, when he was down, he looked at me the way he really looks at women. Pure contempt. We're all stupid fucking cunts who need a man to slap us around and show us what to do. It's probably a good thing I didn't have any more bullets. You know, I scared myself that way, too. I really could have killed him. I mean, not just that I had a gun—I wanted to kill him and I was in the mood to do it. Shooting him in the foot felt so good I didn't know what to think. But I know that if I'd had another round and you had pointed to his head and nodded, I'd have killed him and enjoyed it, too.''

''I acted worse than you did last night.''

She laughed. ''Putting those oxen outside? After they beat you half to death and nearly finished you off?''

''Shooting him in the foot was business. There was a reason for it. What I did was just mean.''

She looked over at me. ''You're pretty hard on yourself, aren't you?''

I considered this. ''And what about you?''

''Huh?''

''An attractive young woman, career of her own, making it in the big city, gives everything up to juggle figures in a backwater where the average age is sixty and where Red is probably one of the most eligible men around.''

''So it's not LA.''

''It's not anything. What's up here for you?''

''You men. If you were told you'd have to live in my house alone for a year, you'd be trying to figure out a way to get laid within two days.''

''Hey, take it easy. You know I didn't mean it that way. It's just that there're no neighbors, no movies, no TV, no library. Nothing to do in town except go somewhere else. What kind of a life is it?''

''A quiet one. And a simple one. And it suits me fine.''

''What happened in LA to change you? I mean, you must have liked it to stay for so many years.''

''At the time, I did. But passing thirty, and Dan,

and Mom being alone—well, LA suited me for a while and then it didn't. What can I say?''

We drove in a companionable silence for some miles after that. What could anyone say? At least she picked a place instead of just staying on where she happened to be born, like a barnacle. The motion of the car made my dizziness worse, but my headache receded to the point where I could think about food again.

We decided to stop for lunch at a Howard Johnson's about twenty miles north of Reading on Route 61. I sat across from her in a booth, still wearing my parka.

I was vaguely nauseated, but I ordered anyway. Even sitting in the car I had felt my blood sugar falling. I put some ice in my coffee and waited for it to cool.

"Mr. Garrett?''

"Call me Dave.''

"Are we in any danger?''

"Not from the Pagans. If they were going to come back they would have rousted up their buddies and been around last night. But as for the people that sent them, yes. Not sitting here in the middle of a public place, and I'm pretty certain we weren't followed. But yes, there's risk.''

"I've been looking in my mirror the whole time. I'm certain we weren't followed.''

"I've been checking, too. It's easy when you have to sit the way I do. But it's hard to be sure. Not seeing the tail is either good or very bad.''

"Go on.''

"The tail can be so good you never see it.''

"How?''

"It's a question of resources and skill. A good tail might involve five cars. All in radio or phone contact. You have a close tail that keeps you in sight, and someone else farther back. They trade off every few miles. You have a car in front who can pull over and keep an eye out if the boys in the back lose touch. And he may drop back and trade off covering the rear himself from time to time. But my experience is, in a multicar tail, the man in front is usually in charge. You have the likely destinations staked out so that if everybody screws up or the suspect gets suspicious, you can pick it up again. If you're confident you know where the suspect is going you can have changes of cars waiting along the route, too, but that's pretty sophisticated."

"Have you ever done a tail like that?"

I laughed. "No, no. All I've done is read about tails like that. But when there's a lot at stake, like the DEA following a courier in a drug case through a major city, it's done like that. The people I tail are mainly cheating husbands and wives going to visit their squeezes. All they can think about is how horny they are. I could probably sit in the passenger's seat and not be noticed."

"You've been an investigator how long?"

"Two years."

"So how do you know all this?"

"When I started out I did a lot of criminal work. You pick up a lot of police procedures. Then when I did personal injury work, I was the lawyer and the investigator rolled into one. The issues were mainly traffic accidents, but it got my mind working in the right channels. Also my domestic work involved knowing about investigations. And I had a lot of friends on the force, especially detectives. When I lost my license and told them what I wanted to do, they spent a lot of time answering questions. The rest is on-the-job training.''

"How could you make friends with the police if you were a defense lawyer?''

"I was fair with them on the witness stand; never pulled anything crooked. I never made a claim I couldn't prove. And I never allowed a client to perjure himself. And besides, the lawyers that the police really hate are the DAs anyway. They see the defense lawyers as just doing their job. They respect them for it. But when the DA tells them he's dropping their prosecution they go apeshit. They think they've been stabbed in the back.''

Our food arrived. I ate it, but an hour later I couldn't remember what it was.

"You know your job very well, Dave.''

"Not well enough.''

"Oh?''

"If I did, I wouldn't be sitting here hurting and I wouldn't have needed you to wipe my ass for me. I was sloppy last night and it was pure luck it didn't get me—and you—killed.''

"They caught you by surprise.''

"Pearl Harbor was a surprise. That's an explanation, not an excuse. I should never have let it happen. But I was so far out in the woods and it was so late I got sloppy. I should have secured the door behind me—blocked it with a couple chairs or some boxes—and kept my gun with me. Simple precautions. But they take thinking, and I'd shut down. Too eager to see what was inside.''

"You're being too hard on yourself. Didn't you lock the door behind you?"

"Sure. But your lock is so simple that anyone who seriously wanted in could have gotten past it."

"I couldn't have."

"It's the people who could get past that lock silently that you need to be scared of."

We paid our bill and left. Standing next to her car I scanned the parking lot carefully. I didn't see anything. Somehow, I wasn't comforted.

The junkyard was on Route 322 a few miles west of Honeybrook, near the Lancaster County line. We were on top of a ridgeline, and the cold westerly howled past our ears. The sun was casting long shadows, but there was plenty of light left.

Ziemer's directions had been perfect. The junkyard was on the south side of the highway, about half a mile west of the Lanchester landfill. I was surprised at how small it was; not more than fifty or seventy-five cars, and no fence. No sign or office, either. The owner probably only dealt with people he knew.

We walked around until we spotted it, sitting by itself at the rear next to a line of hemlocks. Except for the rust, it looked much the same as in the police photos. Sheets of plastic had been taped tightly over the driver's window and the passenger's window. Walking slowly on the uneven ground, I looked at it from all sides.

"Why would they store the car out here and not at the police station?" Lisa asked.

"Takes up room. For a long time. And anyone who was interested in it for the wrong reasons would know where it was."

"But couldn't something happen to it out here, too?"

"Something random, sure. Someone could steal a wheel or something. But no one out here is going to want the fender or the important pieces. And even if they did, the police still have their pictures. Keeping the actual car around is pure backup."

As I squatted down to get a close look at the bullet holes, my dizziness returned with full force. I closed my eyes and concentrated on breathing evenly, hoping Lisa wouldn't notice. When I was able to open them again, I saw that the edges of the holes showed the same angle that the strings indicated. The rounds had come from the rear and slightly above the fender.

"Lisa, how fast were you going when the other car pulled up?"

"Forty, maybe a little faster. We weren't in any hurry."

"Did you brake hard?"

"Yeah. But not to the point of leaving skid marks, if that's what you want to know."

"Did you brake before or after the shot that broke the window?"

"It happened so fast, the shot was before I could get the car slowed down much."

I nodded and walked around the car again, taking pictures as I went. I stopped when I reached the rear. A small hole, not much bigger than a pencil, had been punched into one of the lenses of the taillights. Ignoring the dizziness, I got on my hands and knees to study it. The lens wasn't cracked around the hole; it was a clean punch. And from what I could tell the bulb inside looked intact. I took four close-ups and one longer shot showing the taillight and the license plate.

I checked the rest of the car and found nothing. We got back in Lisa's car. I told her to turn right and head for West Chester. Dusk was falling and she switched on her lights.

"So where in West Chester?"

"I want to visit Todd Brogan. He gave me directions; they start once we get to town."

"Was he a friend of Dan's?"

"Yeah."

She nodded. "So did you find anything?"

I hesitated. Normally I don't discuss investigations in progress with the client, especially when all I have is a suspicion. But she'd been straight with me. I owed her.

"Do you want to know?"

"Of course."

"The left rear taillight has a small hole in it. I can't be sure, but I think it's old. From the time of the shooting."

"What does that mean?"

"It helps prove your brother was murdered by a pro."

"Go on."

"If you want to tail someone, and you're pretty confident that they don't know they're going to be followed, you can make your job easier. You take a pencil or pen or something of that size and punch a small hole in the taillight. When it's on you see a small white light in the middle of the red. Then you can drop back farther and not have to worry about losing your man in traffic."

"So Dan and I were followed all day?"

"Possibly. It wouldn't do any good in the day-time, of course, but someone may have followed you most of the day and done this when dusk was coming on. Look, you need to tell me exactly where you two went."

"I was staying at Mom's. He left from his place and came directly there. We had breakfast together."

"He didn't go to his office first?"

"No. It was a Sunday, and I was supposed to leave on Tuesday. He'd worked most of Saturday so that he could take the whole day off."

"What time did he arrive?"

"Nine or nine-thirty. We ate and left about ten-thirty or eleven."

"Did anyone know where you were going?"

"We told Mom I was going clothes shopping. I said 'the outlets' but not where. We could have gone to Allentown or somewhere in lower Bucks or even over to New Jersey for all she knew."

"Why was Dan going along?"

"It was our only chance to see each other. Plus, he would shop for things of his own. Books, re-cords, things like that."

"Go on."

"We went by the turnpike to the Ephrata exit and then went north to Reading. We shopped the outlets till two or three and then drove straight to the Park City Mall. We had a snack and shopped there till five, when it closed. Then we drove east on Route Thirty through the tourist area. We took back roads and watched the buggies for an hour. Then we cut north to New Holland and took the main road east to Morgantown. We got there a little after seven. I remember thinking we were in no hurry because we still had an hour till our reservation."

"Any stops after Park City?"

"No."

"Was your car in the middle of the lot there?"

"Oh, yes. Lots of cars and people around."

"That probably saved you two from getting killed right there. They probably had been following Dan since he left his apartment, waiting for their chance. The car wasn't alone until you got onto Route Ten."

"We were alone in the Amish country."

I shook my head. "Not alone enough. You think of Lancaster County as rural, but every square inch is in use. It's one big factory, but because it's a factory for plants and animals instead of machines, everybody thinks it's wilderness. There are people everywhere—you're never out of sight of farmhouses or some little town. There's very little secluded country unless you know exactly where to look. Too risky from their point of view. They'd waited all day, they could afford to wait for a better opportunity. Especially because the car was so conspicuous with that taillight."

"Does the hole in the light help our case?"

"Maybe. The insurance company's lawyer is going to rip me up on cross—it could have been put there yesterday; it could have been there because of some innocent reason, like a piece of gravel, a year before the shooting; it could be damage from the shooting. It could have happened any time in the last seven years. I can't prove that it was done the day of the shooting; that's the weak point. And the worst part is that the police didn't pick it up."

"So?"

"The inference will be that if they didn't see it then, it was because it wasn't there then."

"But wouldn't that really be accusing you of putting it there?"

"Yes, but they won't put it that way; they'll be more sophisticated. They'll say I've misinterpreted the significance of finding this hole seven years later, something benign like that. But if the judge is going our way anyway, this will help."

"It all sounds so iffy."

"Now you know why trial lawyers drink so much."

West Chester hadn't changed since the last time I'd visited; a slum trying to convince itself it was a suburb. As we drove through the downtown, a few trendy neo-Victorian shops with hand-carved signs thrust out at us from a background of grimy brick storefronts.

We turned onto Brogan's street and parked in his driveway. It was a pleasant, middle-class neighborhood with old shade trees, generous setbacks to the houses, and no sidewalks. Brogan's own house was a two-story brick colonial with well-tended shrubbery. And, I saw as I approached the porch, two days' uncollected newspapers.

Going up the three porch steps brought on the dizziness again, and when I leaned against the wall I used my right arm by mistake. At least the pain from my ribs took away the dizziness.

"Go ahead and ring the bell if you want," I said disgustedly. "It isn't going to do any good."

After we satisfied ourselves that no one was home, I had Lisa walk around. I wasn't in shape for it just then, mentally or physically. I had a bad feeling that this wasn't just a missed appointment. Someone had warned him off. I decided to keep it to myself.

"There's no car in the garage," Lisa reported. "A couple of inside lights are on in the back, plus the exterior floodlights. Everything is locked up tight. Looks like someone didn't want to talk to us."

So much for keeping my own counsel. "Yeah."

"So now where?"

"Take me to a phone booth. We'll decide after that."

We retraced our steps and found a phone at a convenience store near Route 100. Lisa gave me all her change and waited in the car with the engine running. I let it ring twice, hung up, and called again. The phone was picked up but no one answered.

"Yo, this is Garrett."

"From where?"

"A phone booth."

"Okay. You got the bucks, I got the dope."

"One large."

"This is good stuff, man. You'll want to know."

"How good?"

"Ten large."

"Fuck, no. You crazy?" I asked.

"No shit, man. I got expenses. This is a three-way split."

"I never paid more than three."

"I never had anything this good for you."

"Five or forget it." Actually I didn't mind the bill, especially since it wasn't coming out of my pocket. But he expected me to haggle.

"When?"

"Tomorrow. The usual way."

"Okay. The dope is, Wilson was doing work for the big boys. Not an inside man, but getting into some heavy cases."

"That much I knew."

"Fuck you man. I bet you didn't know this. They offed him."

"I've figured that, too."

"You know why?"

"He'd taken something of theirs."

"But you don't know what."

"That's what the five's for, if it's worth it at all."

"He was doin' a case, drug case, for one of their people. The dude gave Wilson a bag with a hundred g's in it for safekeeping. Then the guy gets killed; he's a middle-level coke dealer; one of his customers tried to strong-arm him and they shot it out. Wilson keeps the money, thinking nobody knows. But the big boys figure it out. End of story."

"You earned your money. But don't think that next time I'll pay five hundred for the weather report. This is a one-time deal."

"Same for me, man. This is too heavy."

On that note, we hung up. I was tired and disgusted and in pain. My headache was back and my food wasn't sitting well.

And as I walked back to Lisa's car I saw a white beam of light peeping out of the left rear taillight.

11

SUNDAY, 6:00 P.M.

I got into the car as quickly as I could and hoped that no one had seen me break stride. I found myself touching the .357 for reassurance. Hard thinking has saved a lot more lives than hardware; but the cold chunk of metal felt good anyway.

"What's the matter?" she asked.

"Pull out slowly onto Route One-Hundred north."

Evening traffic was fairly heavy. I looked back and then in front, wondering which lights had our names on them.

"Lisa, we've got a problem. Someone has marked our taillight, like Dan's."

"When?"

"I don't know. It could have been at the restaurant near Reading; we weren't watching the car every minute. Or it could have been while you were parked at my office yesterday. Or while you were at your mom's."

She looked in the mirror. "Is anybody following?"

"In this traffic, no way to tell. And if they're good, we'll never know it."

"What do they want?"

"They might want to kill us; they might be just following us to see where we go; they might be trying to sell us a subscription to *Boy's Life*. Let's work on the most pessimistic assumption."

"Okay, what do we do?"

"When you get to Thirty, turn left and head west, back toward Lancaster. We need some elbow room. It's too easy for them to follow us in traffic."

"But if we're alone with them?"

"We're going to have to stop sometime. And we sure can't go to my place or your place. Even if we lost them on the way, they may be staked out."

"What about going to the police?"

"If they would be so obliging as to pull in behind us when we get to the station, fine. But assuming they don't, that they just lose themselves until we come out again, what do we do? Hang around the police station till noon tomorrow and hope we don't get hit on the drive to Philly? Ask the police to arrest suspicious-looking cars, whatever that means? We don't even know who to describe, or how many there are."

"I still think the police could help."

"At most they could help detain one or two of the cars. If this is a serious tail—and there's no way of knowing how big it is—if we don't get all of them, then all we've done is make it worse. They'd know we're wise to them. If they mean us harm, they'd move in right away then."

"Okay."

"In your purse, do you have any cotton balls?"

"In my overnight bag. There on the backseat. In a little plastic bag along with my nail polish and the nail polish remover."

I fumbled around in the dark until I found them. I moistened four with my mouth, put two in my own ears, and gave the others to her.

"What's this for?"

"Ear protection. Put them in."

"Okay, but why?"

I spoke slowly and carefully to make sure she could hear. "If something happens it'll happen real fast. There won't be a second chance to explain. If someone pulls up alongside who means trouble, I'm going to have to shove this gun right in front of your face and shoot out the window, past your head. I'll be firing a couple of inches from your left ear. This is a much more powerful gun than your twenty-two. It's going to sound like the end of the world."

"This is like a bad dream I can't wake up from."

"At least this time we know what's coming."

The traffic thinned after we turned onto Route 30, but there were always three or four sets of lights behind us, plus a couple in front. Every so often someone would pass and my mouth would turn dry. I kept the gun in my lap, ready to shoot left-handed if necessary. A pair of hot-rodding teenagers came very close to death when they pulled alongside and matched our speed. Then the passenger smiled at Lisa and they pulled away.

We avoided the four-lane bypass around Downingtown and went through the city; it would be too easy to make a hit on a deserted, limited-access road.

"I've got a plan," I said, speaking a little louder than normal.

She was all business. "Let's hear it."

"We're not far from the Welsh Mountains. I have a friend who has a cabin there. He only uses it in the summers; I'm sure it's empty now. No one will be expecting us to go there."

"What's the Welsh Mountains?"

"In eastern Lancaster County, near Blue Ball. It's a series of wooded ridges, pretty steep by Lancaster County standards. Very undeveloped, or at least it was until recently. Before the Civil War it was a stop on the Underground Railroad. It was settled mostly by the descendants of escaped slaves. Very poor and remote area. Few roads. Now yuppies are buying it up for country houses. But my friend's place is well hidden. If we can get there we'll be safe. And we don't have much choice."

"You think my mom's is being watched, too?"

"Probably. And even if they're not watching it now, you can bet they'll start if we shake the tail. There's nowhere else to go."

"Let's do it."

"Pull into the next self-service gas station you see."

"We've got plenty."

"We need to buy a few seconds. We can't possibly lose them with the taillight as it is. Your nail polish, is it red?"

"Close enough."

"You're going to have to do this. I don't trust my balance. When we pull in, shut off the lights and get out. Take the nail polish with you. Start pumping the gas and open the trunk. Make like

you're looking for something. The left lens is the
damaged one. Reach inside the trunk and feel along
the wires to the base of the bulb. Pull on the base
till it comes out. Then paint the bulb red; cover it
completely. Then put it back in place. Be sure it's
in solid. If the light doesn't come on we'll be even
more conspicuous. Pay for the gas and get back in.
Start the engine but don't touch the brakes or turn
on the lights. And buckle your seat belt tight.''

''What's the point?''

''They don't know we're onto them. The tail may
be loose right now. If they can't see their indicator
it may take them by surprise. If we can get ten
seconds on them at the right point it may be
enough.''

Another five minutes up the road, at the intersection with Route 340, we saw a convenience store
with pumps. The view ahead was good. I looked
behind me as we pulled in; several cars went by.
One pair of headlights pulled into a parking lot
about a hundred yards back and went out. Up
ahead, a car stopped just before the 340 intersection. He was good; he was positioned to follow us
either way. I could feel the gun becoming slick in
my hand.

Lisa opened her door and bounced over to the
pumps as if her biggest worry was the amount of
the discount for cash. She started pumping. Then,
making a show of biting her thumbnail, she opened
the trunk and rummaged around. For about a minute I heard nothing; Jesus, couldn't she find the
bulb, or get it out? Then she paid for the gas and
got in again.

''What went wrong?''

"Nothing. All done."

"I let out my breath. "Thanks. Good job. Ready?"

She nodded.

"There's one about a hundred yards back and one up ahead at the intersection. When I say, pull out and go down to the turn. Take it easy. After you turn onto Three-Forty west, hit it and go like hell."

She started the engine. Her foot, I noticed, stayed clear of the brake. A good person to have in a tight spot with you.

Two cars passed by close together; five more were coming up. The gap was no more than three car lengths.

"Now!"

She hit the lights and shot smoothly into the space. The car right behind us honked, and my heart jumped. But the car I was really interested in, the one in the parking lot, was stuck in the parking lot, waiting for the five cars to get by. If Lisa did the job right, we'd just be one of half a dozen sets of identical taillights.

I got a good look at the car at the intersection, a dark late-model American car. Thunderbird. One occupant. Most likely the man in charge.

Lisa slowed, made the turn without signaling, floored it, and dropped down a gear. The engine howled and I was snapped back in my seat. My ribs hurt, again, but I kept it to myself. Behind me, I saw a single pair of headlights: the Thunderbird.

"We've lost the one who was behind us. He must have overshot the intersection looking for us."

The speedometer passed sixty and then seventy

but the Thunderbird kept gaining. We were getting to the limit of what Lisa's car would do and it wasn't near enough.

"Take the next road you come to."

"Left or right?"

"Doesn't matter."

We were going too fast to make the first one, but Lisa had a glimpse of the next one before we got there. She stood on the brakes, threw us into a left-hand skid, and made the turn at thirty. The shoulder strap cut into my ribs, but I didn't care. She pushed it to the floor and we roared up a long hill at seventy. The car rattled and the wind whistled through the cracks, but over all the other noise I could clearly hear the engine laboring. We weren't doing it any good.

"He's behind us, but farther back," I said. "Oh, goddamn!"

"What?"

"There's somebody else behind him. A lot farther back."

"The one from the parking lot?"

"Maybe. Maybe a third car."

I was still looking back when we crested the hill. "Shit!" Lisa screamed. I turned around. There was nothing at all in front of us except the night sky. The hill dropped off sharply on the other side and we were airborne. "Jesus!" I yelled. "Hold her steady!" The time we were in the air couldn't have been long, but it was enough time to sweat. What if we broke something when we hit, or lost control? They'd be on us before we had time for a good prayer. We crashed heavily onto the road and a metallic *thunk* reverberated through the car. My ribs screamed in protest as I bounced into the door handle and then into the dashboard. We bounced into the air again and then down, but not so heavily. Lisa fought the wheel and kept going. Her foot never left the gas. "Feels okay!" she yelled. A groan came from the right front, but neither of us said anything. Either the car would hold together or it wouldn't, and there was nothing we could do about it.

"Hey, look up ahead!" she said.

The road went down the hill, curved to the right and went up the next hill. But at the bottom, on the left, were some lights. They were too close together for houses, and there were too many for a farm. I could see the dark outline of a large low building. Then I recognized what it was.

"It's a sewage treatment plant," I explained. "If there's an open gate and if you can't see them when we get there, kill your lights and turn in."

The plant seemed huge when we reached the bottom of the hill. It was floodlit and we could see that the gate was open. As we approached, Lisa shut off the lights. I looked back.

"Still okay."

She skidded through the gate and drove around the back of the main building. Then she turned around so that we were facing back toward the exit. "Are we safe?" she asked.

"For a couple of minutes. They'll go by, sure enough. At least the first one will. But as soon as they realize they've lost us they'll backtrack. How long that will be, I don't know. Depends on the terrain on the other side. If it's pretty open they'll be starting back in thirty seconds. And this is the only place we could be. They might even send in one of the trailing cars to check this place out now, so we've got to get out of here pretty quick.''

"Back the way we came?''

"For the moment. Look, we need to disguise our lights. You have yellow parking lights in the grill, right?''

"Yes.''

"Go punch them out, and one of the headlights, too. Take—'' She jumped out of the car before I could hand her one of my gloves. Without hesitation she picked up a rock and pushed it through one parking light, then the other, and then the right headlight. Glass crunched on the pavement as she walked back to the car. When she got behind the wheel, blood was running freely down her right hand.

"Jesus, Lisa, you didn't need—'' She shook her head impatiently. She was right; there was no point in talking about it. I shut up and watched the road.

A pair of headlights—the Thunderbird—flashed by, climbing the hill. He must have been doing eighty. His brake lights flashed on and then disappeared over the crest. There was no one behind him. "Pull out slowly. No lights.''

We inched out from the building, feeling naked in the floodlights. No cars in either direction. I cracked my window and listened. Except for the jumble of noises from under our own hood it was quiet. "Turn right, keep it under fifty, turn the lights on when you're completely on the road. I'm going to crunch down in the seat in case they're counting occupants. Keep me informed.''

It hurt like hell to get down on the floor. I could

only breathe in shallow pants. We had barely reached the bottom of the hill when she started talking. Her voice was quiet and level. "Okay; there's a car coming over the hill toward us. He took a bounce but he's still coming. He's slowing, slowing; now he's past us. He's gone right past the sewer plant and is going up the next hill. Now he's gone. Now we're back to the big crest; now we're over. Oh, now I can see some more headlights coming up. He's slowing, checking us out, going past. Shit! He's turning around!" I could feel her accelerating.

"Take the first turn anywhere and haul ass." I straightened up; no point in hiding anymore. I looked out the rear window, watching the headlights come around and then point toward us.

She found a right and took it smoothly; she was up to forty when we saw farm buildings up ahead. "Goddamn," she yelled. "We're in a farm lane! No way out!"

I looked up. The lane ended just ahead, in a courtyard formed by a house and a couple of barns. I couldn't see any lights. The lane had a shallow drainage ditch down one side. There was only one option left. "Hit the brakes and stop the car across the lane with my door toward the farm. Then crawl out my side, lie on the ground, and don't move. Try to stay out of sight behind a wheel."

She skidded to a stop just as I'd asked, and I opened the door. Crouching over and trying to ignore the pain, I staggered across the lane and toward the road. I had been thinking of hiding in the drainage pitch, but then I saw a tractor parked near the edge of the field.

As I reached it, a pair of headlights turned into the lane. I lay down on the earth on the far side of the tractor. The ground was cold and uneven, and a couple of fair-size rocks were jutting into my ribs. The headlights came up fast and stopped about twenty yards to my right. The car must have been pointed in the direction of the tractor; the headlights brightened everything around me. I was barely hidden behind the front wheels; from where the driver was, my feet were probably visible. There was no point in changing position; any motion would make things worse. All I could do was hope that his attention was focused on our car.

I closed my eyes and buried my face in the earth, trying to preserve as much of my night vision as I could. I heard a single car door slam. At least he was alone. He left the engine running; even better. Some sound to mask my noise. Then I heard the unmistakable and terrifying sound of a pump-action shotgun being worked. As he got closer I heard the crunch of his shoes on the snow. He was walking fast. This was a pro, and one who wasn't going to waste any time.

His steps approached from my right, moved in front of me and then to my left, clean past the tractor. I took as deep a breath as my ribs permitted and tried to calm myself. The first shot is your best chance, especially at night when everyone's vision is ruined by the flashes once the shooting starts. Once we were both shooting blindly, a pistol against a shotgun at close range—well, there wasn't much point in dwelling on that. I decided to take the time to cock the .357 and shoot single action.

I couldn't afford to let my first shot be anything but my best.

I opened my eyes and extended the gun, bracing my elbows in the earth. Most of the light was off to my right; he and I were both in shadow. In that moment I wasn't dizzy. I didn't have a headache. I wasn't hungry or cold or tired. The only things in my universe were the gun, the target, and my finger on the trigger. I held my gun in my left hand only; using the right for a brace would just punish my ribs more. He was no more than ten yards from me when I cocked my piece.

He was good; he may have sensed my motion as I changed slowly into a firing position. Or maybe he saw a glint of moonlight off the barrel as I aimed. He spun around toward me, lowering his shotgun toward my face.

That was as far as he got. Gripping my piece as hard as I could, I gently touched off the first round. The gun bucked in my hand, and the noise rang in my ears like a thunderclap. The bullet hit him like a two-by-four, flinging him backward. The flash from the muzzle dazzled me. Blindly, I followed up with two more shots. I don't know if either of them hit, but after my third shot he staggered and fell to the ground.

As quickly as I could, I got up and shuffled over to him. I don't know if he was alive or not. Thinking about what I'd done would have to wait; my concern was keeping myself and Lisa alive. I picked up his shotgun, a 12-gauge riot gun with a seven-shot magazine and a folding stock. A lot of people in Vietnam preferred them to M-16s. Putting the shotgun on ''safe,'' I hobbled over to his car and turned out the headlights. There was no point in helping him advertise his location. I glanced around the car; it was equipped with both a cellular phone and a CB. If we were lucky we had a minute and a half to get the hell out of there. Using the shotgun to help steady myself, I headed back to Lisa's car as quickly as I could.

One hand bloody, Lisa helped me into the passenger seat. I didn't even try to spare my ribs; I was too tired and dizzy to care. "Thanks," I said. "Now let's get out of here. Assuming he called in where he was going, the others will be right behind."

"What about him?"

"They'll be here soon enough. They'll take care of him. One way or another."

She made a right onto the main road, then took the next right. This one was a road, not a lane, and we followed it for nearly five miles. Blessedly, it stayed dark and silent behind us the whole way. Finally the road brought us out in a little town named Cambridge. We stopped behind a building for ten minutes. No cars went past.

"So far so good," I said.

"Until tomorrow."

"We'll worry about that tomorrow. It's been a full day already."

"What now?"

"Follow this road. It should run into Gault Road. That'll take us right where we want to go."

"How can you know all these roads?"

"I stay with my friend weekends in the summer. We ride bikes all around here. When you're moving at ten miles an hour there's plenty of time to consider the roads.''

We reached the base of a line of ridges and started up. The farmhouses stopped abruptly once we started climbing, and the bare fields were replaced by stands of scrub pine. I looked back the entire time; there was nothing behind us. After we'd climbed steadily for about five minutes, I told her to slow down.

''Now turn off your headlights and just creep along for a bit. If there's anyone trailing us we haven't seen, this'll flush them out.''

''How could that be, if we can't see them?''

''Infrared. Not very likely, but possible. We have to be really careful. If we lead them to the cabin, there's nowhere else we can go.''

We went a few hundred yards, edging off onto the shoulder a couple of times, till I was satisfied.

''Okay, the road is going to dip down. At the bottom of the dip is a trail to the right. Take it without using your brakes and pull up so there are trees on both sides.''

It was an inelegant turn, but at least she did it without activating the brake lights. Again we waited for several minutes.

''We're alone,'' I said.

''For sure?''

''Sure as I can be.'' She put her head back against the headrest and closed her eyes. I wanted to ask her what she was thinking, then decided not to. ''All right,'' I continued. ''You can use your lights now. Up the trail a bit is a chain across the road. It has a padlock with a combination, four-

four-oh. Lock it up again behind us and drive up
to the cabin.''

After the gate, the trail went into a right-hand
climbing turn. It leveled off at the cabin, in a clearing at the top of the hill. It was a modern log construction with a stone chimney, surrounded by a
split-rail fence. I got the key from under the porch.
Inside, except for the bedroom and bathroom in the
rear, it was one big room, with broad-plank yellow
pine floors.

"This is great," Lisa said. "Does your friend
come here often?"

"In the summer, he and his wife come up for
the weekends. He and his girlfriend use it during
the week. Nobody uses it much in the winter at
all.''

I set down my pistol and pumped the shotgun to
eject the shell. Lisa picked it up and looked at it
carefully. "Doesn't look like much. Not like a bullet, I mean. It's mostly red plastic. Looks like a
firecracker.''

I took it from her and held it between two fingers. "It's double-aught buckshot. A second later
and my mother couldn't have identified me.''

I put the round back into the magazine with the
others, and put on the safety. I turned away so she
wouldn't see how hard my hands were shaking.

I cranked up the heat—it was left at fifty anyway
to keep the pipes from freezing—and looked
through the cupboards. Pickings were slim. Finally
I found some cans of spaghetti. It was the only
thing to eat other than a jar of black olives.

Lisa brought in some wood and went to work
kindling a fire in the massive stone fireplace that

took up most of one wall. By the time I'd finished
my food inventory, she was sitting on her haunches
on a fake bearskin rug in front of the fire. It was
blazing nicely.

"You do good work," I said.

"When you heat with wood you get a lot of practice."

"Come in the bathroom and let me look at your
arm."

Her hand and arm up to the elbow were so covered in blood I couldn't tell a thing. I rolled up her
bloody sweater sleeve and put her arm under luke-
warm water in the sink.

"Holy shit." The back of her hand looked as if
she'd argued with a garbage disposal. A dozen cuts
crisscrossed at different angles. But the worst were
four deep lacerations starting just behind the
knuckles; two of them went almost to the wrist,
and all of them were deep, with flaps of loose skin
clearly visible.

"You're going to have to do the work," she said.
"I can't do this left-handed."

"Can you move the fingers okay?"

She nodded. When I stopped running the water
I saw more bad news; the deep cuts were still
bleeding, and embedded glass glittered in the harsh
bathroom light. "Let me get you a drink."

"I'll be okay. Just get to work."

There were no tweezers in the medicine cabinet,
but fortunately she had brought a pair in her bag. I
worked with my right hand despite the pain it
caused my side; there was no other way. Extracting
the glass was slow work, and concentrating gave
me a terrific headache. Some pieces were round

and easy to see. Others were slivers that only showed up when the light hit them a certain way. Every time I pulled a piece out it caused fresh bleeding. I had to work on one laceration for a while and then move to another till the bleeding in the first one subsided enough for me to see what I was doing. It took the better part of an hour; she never moved a muscle the entire time. "Okay," I said, showing her the bottle of hydrogen peroxide, the only disinfectant we had. "This is going to hurt." She nodded for me to go ahead. I poured the bottle liberally all over her hand. The peroxide foamed and bubbled everywhere it touched raw flesh. Even though it didn't matter now, she still kept her hand perfectly still.

When the bubbling subsided, I wrapped her hand in a thin hand towel and taped it into a rough bandage. "I'll change it again in the morning. I got what I could but you'd better see a doctor when this is over. There was a lot of glass."

"Thanks." She let out a long breath. "I could use that drink now."

I rummaged in the medicine cabinet. My friend was halfway to a hypochondriac, and I found what I was looking for. "Look, here are some sleeping pills. Take something before you hit the hay. That thing's going to hurt. You might as well try and sleep through it."

I found a couple of bottles of champagne in the refrigerator, left over from Lord knows what tryst, and filled a jelly jar for her. "Take it easy for a few minutes. I'm going to take a shower. Then you can take one and we can have some dinner."

My clothes were in a sad state. Everything was

filthy. My shirt was blotchy pink from diluted bloodstains, three of the buttons were missing, and the right sleeve was half torn off at the shoulder. Somehow, at some point, I'd ripped one knee out of my pants. Even my undershirt was torn and bloodied. When I was in the shower the tape washed off my side. I took one look and decided not to look again.

I put on one of the bathrobes hanging behind the bathroom door and hung my clothes up to dry. There was no razor; I would just have to let my beard go for another day. While Lisa took her shower I finished assembling our dinner. She came back wearing the other bathrobe, and we ate sitting on the bearskin next to the fire.

When we were finished I threw another log on the fire while she cleared away the plates. She turned off the lights, came back with some pillows, and put them behind me. Then she shrugged off her bathrobe, lay down against me, and pulled the robe over both of us.

"What are we going to do tomorrow?" she asked.

"We're safe if we don't do anything but just go to the hearing. They don't know where we are now, so if we take a back way to Philly, they'd have to get really lucky to pick us up. And once we get to the courthouse there's no problem. There's security and metal detectors and cops everywhere."

"That makes me feel better."

"How are you doing?" I asked.

"It'll be okay; the tendons aren't damaged."

"Your days as a hand model are over."

She held up her right hand for a moment and

then used it to open my robe and rub my chest. "It's all been like a dream," she said softly. "In a way, everything since Dan died has. But the last two days especially. If I didn't hurt so much I wouldn't be sure it was really happening."

"It is, believe me."

"What are you thinking?"

"About a man in a farm lane. I wonder how it seems to him."

"You shouldn't think about that."

"No, you're right," I said. I was looking at the ceiling. At that moment Lisa seemed far away and the man in the lane seemed very close. "It doesn't do anybody any good. But this is new for me. I mean, I know guns because I have to know my job. Like I have to know about how to do a surveillance or how to trace skips. But I've never killed anything. Before this, I mean. Even in the war, I never killed anything myself. I don't even hunt."

"He could have been the one that killed Dan."

"If it wasn't him, it might as well have been." Neither of us said anything for a while. "You know the worst part of killing him?"

"Stop it. You had to do it."

"The worst part isn't that he's dead; he probably deserved worse. It's that I'm the one who did it. I know that I can kill. I don't like knowing that about myself."

"That's what I learned last night with that biker. I guess we're even. Let's not talk anymore."

She put her cheek against my shoulder and kissed me gently on the neck. I kissed her back, a long time, and put my arm around her. With my right hand I traced the line of her jaw. She closed her eyes and pressed her cheek against my palm. Then her left hand slid down my chest and untied the knot in my robe.

"You know," I said, "I've never done this with a client before."

"Sorry to break your streak."

Her fingers moved down my stomach to my groin. We were ready for each other. She threw a leg over me and guided me inside. As she straightened up, straddling me, her robe fell away from her shoulders. When she threw it clear, her hair shadowed her face. She pulled it back, tying it into a rough knot. "It can get in the way," she explained. As she tied it, I watched the line of her body from her arm running down her side, narrowing at the waist and flaring out a little at the hip. It was the way I'd thought she would look, smooth and graceful and athletic. Very gently, I ran one finger all along it.

The firelight outlined her body in flickering reds and golds. I ran my hands over her thighs, up her sides, and over her breasts. "You are beautiful," I said slowly.

She looked away. "I'm glad you think so."

"More than beautiful. Exquisite."

"Now you're teasing me."

"Absolutely not." I put a hand on each side of her waist. "Of all the places in the world I could be right now, I can't think of one I'd rather be than right here."

She laughed. "My God, you must be Irish."

"Hardly. Russian Jew. And a very secular one at that."

She began moving her hips slowly back and

forth, then more urgently. "As much," she gasped, "as I'd like to continue this conversation, it feels too good to wait. Don't worry about me. This one's for you." There was no finesse in the way she rode me that first time; it was quick and sweaty and more than a little rough. When she sensed I was ready to come she started contracting herself around me till she milked me dry.

After we finished she still sat astride me, watching. "Was it okay?"

I brought her face down to me and kissed her. Some loose strands of hair fell in my face. "You've got a lot of nerve sounding worried. It was wonderful."

"It's been a while."

I thought of the vibrator and the unopened box of condoms in her dresser. "I feel badly now, about going through your personal things."

"You pick a funny time to get embarrassed." She slid off me. "How do you feel about having your dick sucked?"

"I'll have to think about that for a tenth of a second. Okay, then. All right, I suppose. Jesus Christ, what are—how did you learn to do *that*?"

I was forty-four years old, my side hurt, I had a headache that felt like the end of the world, and I'd drunk more champagne than was good for me. And none of it mattered. In a few minutes she was back on top of me and we were making love again.

The second time was hers. With my ribs I couldn't move much, but she didn't mind; she set the pace. She was in no hurry to finish. Neither was I.

12

MONDAY, 5:00 A.M.

The fire was dying when I awoke. For a few minutes I lay there watching the play of the firelight on the ceiling. Lisa was burrowed against my left side, her left leg thrown over mine and her breasts pressed against my chest. The firelight played on the curves of her body. Her breathing was deep and regular, and she was snoring, just a little. Her hair, next to my nose, smelled of sex and pine smoke and shampoo.

I wanted to turn over, but that was not possible without either disturbing Lisa or rolling onto my damaged side, so I stayed still. In addition to my ribs and my headache, I had a new discomfort, this one in my rear. The second time, after Lisa was too exhausted to continue, she'd helped me over the top with a finger against my prostate. I shifted slightly to keep the sore spot off the bearskin.

I tried to sleep and failed. I started thinking about Lisa and pressed my lips gently against her hair. But that was a luxury. There was a case and it wasn't finished. I stared at the ceiling and tried to put the pieces together. I studied the knotholes in the ceiling, watching the play of the firelight. The holes were scattered randomly; here were three small ones close together forming a triangle, over there was a pair, and directly above me, one large one in isolation. Like the case, there was no pattern. The more I tried to impose one the more disjointed it seemed.

What is thinking, really? How can you explain how it is that you come to understand something? You try to teach a child that two and two are four; he looks at you blankly at first, and then if you're lucky, his face lights up and he gets it. But there's nothing in between—either the connection is made or it isn't.

That was what happened to me in the quiet hour before dawn. One moment the case was as obscure as ever; the next moment I had the solution. I can't pretend for a moment that I rationally followed it from *A* to *B* to *Z;* just suddenly it was there. It wasn't a question of making the knotholes do what I wanted; it was seeing the pattern that had always been there. The only reason it had been hard to see was because I'd refused to see it.

"Lisa," I whispered. "Lisa, honey, we need to get up."

Initially there was no response. Either she was a very sound sleeper or the combination of champagne and sleeping pills had hit her pretty hard. "Lisa," I said, louder. "We have to go."

Her face appeared, her eyes half open. "Huh?"

"We need to get to Philadelphia."

"It's the middle of the night."

"It's going to be dawn in an hour. We have things to do. Now."

"Let's fuck some more. Or sleep."

"Later. There'll be plenty of time for that later. But we have to go now. It's important."

"Those pills. Arghh." But at least she was awake.

I was so tired I could barely move, but I managed to get her leg off me and stand up. The room danced around, but not as badly as yesterday. My headache had receded to the point where I could work around it. I dressed while Lisa struggled to wake up. Then I changed her bandage and checked outside while she dressed. The engine hadn't been tampered with. I felt as safe as I could expect to. I put the shotgun in the backseat under a blanket and the pistol back in my pocket.

Lisa came out rubbing her eyes. Despite the cold her jacket was unbuttoned. Her feet were barely moving. "Want me to drive?" she offered gamely.

"Thanks, I'm better today. And you're still sleepy. If you'll just do the gate for me on the way out that'll be fine. Then you can just go back to sleep."

She took me up on it; by the time we reached Route 897 and headed north toward the turnpike, she was asleep.

Shortly after six I pulled into the Valley Forge rest stop and found a phone booth with a directory. I put in my quarters and a sleepy male voice answered.

"Hello?"

"Leo Strasnick?"

"Yes. Who is this? Do you know what time it is?"

"This is Dave Garrett, Mr. Strasnick. And it's time to die."

The line was silent for the space of half a dozen heartbeats. "What are you talking about? And who are you? Aren't you—"

"You know exactly what I mean and who I am. And you have one slim chance to save your miserable ass. The chickens have come home to roost. Meet me in the parking lot of the King of Prussia shopping center in half an hour. Don't be late and be sure you come alone."

"I can't get there that fast."

"If you hurry you can." I couldn't afford to give him any time to organize himself.

"It's a huge lot. What if I miss you?"

"Then you'll be dead. But out of deference to your lifestyle, we'll meet at the main entrance to Bloomingdale's." I hung up.

Lisa was still sleeping, so I got a big coffee and sat with her, keeping the engine running so she'd be warm. I twisted the wrong way buckling my seat belt, and my ribs renewed their complaint. The coffee brought back the pounding in the back of my head, but at least it brought me fully awake. I would need my wits today, I knew. I was hurting and exhausted and the worst was still ahead.

I finished my coffee and drove the ten minutes to the mall. Although the sky was starting to lighten in the east, it was still fully dark. I parked in the middle of the vast parking lot, about a hundred yards from the Bloomingdale's entrance, with the car pointed toward the nearest exit. The lot was well illuminated, but there were no other cars in sight.

"Lisa, wake up. It's time."

She breathed heavily once and opened her eyes. She looked around. "I'm getting tired of asking this, but what's the plan? It's too early to shop."

"I'm going to meet with Leo Strasnick in a minute. You have to be backup."

"Strasnick? Danny's old partner? What for?"

"There isn't time to explain now. Just take it for granted he's dangerous." I handed her the shotgun. "When he parks, roll your window down and sit with the gun sitting up so he can see it. Have you ever fired a pump shotgun before?"

"No. Just that twenty-two pistol."

"It's easy enough to use. Right now it's absolutely safe. If there's any trouble, put your hand here on the slide and pump it back once, as hard as you can, then forward again. That will carry a shell from the magazine into the chamber. Then press this button here behind the trigger to the left so that the red is showing. That button is the safety; when you can see the red, the safety is off and you can fire. Point it at his car and put the stock back hard against your shoulder. Then pull the trigger. It'll kick pretty hard, so hold on tight. You can reload by working the slide again, if you need to. There are seven shots. When you're finished, hide the gun under the blanket and get the hell back to North Carbon. If you go by a river or a lake, throw the thing in."

"What about you?"

"If there's trouble I'll be dead already."

"Do you have to do this?"

"It's this or spend the rest of our lives like we spent the last two days."

A black Mercedes sedan with tinted windows pulled into the parking lot at that moment, roaring past us, and stopped about a hundred yards away. Opening my car door and standing with the door between me and him, I motioned for him to come closer. Then I motioned him to my right so that Lisa could have a clear shot. When he was about twenty-five yards away, I nodded and his engine died.

I swallowed and stepped clear of my car. The only sound was my steps on the concrete. I tried not to think that at any moment one of those black windows could roll down and leave me staring down the muzzle of a gun. I also didn't like the idea of the tinted windows; Lisa wouldn't be able to see anything. But there was nothing to be done.

I walked slowly around to the passenger's side and opened the door. Strasnick was there, his hair tousled, wearing a navy blazer with no tie. His hands were on the wheel and he was alone.

"Strasnick, before I get in I set the ground rules. See the woman in my car? See the gun? It's a police riot gun, and if anything funny happens it'll shred your tires, your sheet metal, your glass, and you, too. So play it straight."

I got in and shut the door.

"I have no intention of harming you or anything else, Mr. Garrett. And I don't like threats. As a matter of fact, I don't know why I didn't just call the police and report—" I hit him with a short right jab. It was awkwardly thrown, but I put as much into it as I could; his head snapped back and banged into the window with a satisfying noise. When he recovered, he was bleeding from the corner of his mouth. My side hurt like hell but it was worth it.

"That's for trying to bullshit me. I've come too far to fuck around with you."

He sat silent, waiting.

"You know where that riot gun comes from? You know your man that didn't come back last night? I took it away from him."

"My man? What are you talking about?"

"Okay. You shut up and I'll explain it to you." My headache was reaching new heights, so strong I could barely concentrate, and I wished I'd taken some more aspirin. Then I thought of Lisa and her hand and stopped feeling sorry for myself.

"Wilson was tired of working for the mob. I don't know if he was scared, or fed up, or what, but he didn't need the money badly enough to keep on doing it. You did. He was an unhappy guy for lots of reasons, you're right about that. But he really did want out of the partnership—because you weren't willing to change. You kept bringing him those cases and he had to take them as long as he was in the firm."

My head was pounding and I wanted to rub my temples, but I didn't want to let him see it. "And then the hundred thousand came in; it must have looked pretty good to you. Back in those days, tax-free, it was a year's income, or more. When the client died, you took it and hoped you'd never hear about it. Wilson wanted no part of it; he said you were crazy. Am I right?"

Strasnick was scared, but he kept his composure. "Only a little. You're very badly misinformed. I've nothing to hide. Dan's representatives are free to check the accounts. There was a large fee, as you say, just before he disappeared. The client deposited a substantial retainer and then died. Dan declined his share—he said I was entitled to the whole thing for bringing in the client. And a share of that money was spent on upgrading the office, from which we all benefited, by the way. That's all there is to say. Mr. Garrett, for a former practitioner, you have some very simpleminded ideas about a law practice."

"I have some simpleminded ideas about how the books can be cooked. So it wasn't tax-free—no difference. You made up a receipt for the money, ran it through the firm as income to avoid the IRS getting on your ass, and kept it yourself. It squared you with the feds, but it didn't help you with the people who really matter. They found out somehow that their man had left the money with your firm, and they asked for it back. And that's when you made your move. You decided to ingratiate yourself with them and get rid of your partner at the same time. You told them he took it."

"That's preposterous. There's not a shred of evidence that it happened that way."

"Bullshit. *They* know very well what you told them. And they know how you lied to them about me and this case."

"What are you talking about?"

A minor leap. "You told someone I know that I was looking for Wilson's killers, which I wasn't. You knew perfectly well I was just establishing that the man hadn't been heard from in seven years; I wasn't looking for anything else. Why lie, unless you were afraid of what I'd find? And why send the muscle out to Lisa Wilson's house?''

''What?''

''I thought they were from the big boys, but I was wrong. You have some connections of your own. You must still do plenty of mob work; it's just that now you've upgraded to a better class of referrals. Helping to arrange buyouts of legit businesses, infiltrate unions, launder money, things like that. You know names of your own now. You called those boys out to North Carbon yourself. You wanted them to trash the house; maybe that would scare Lisa off. It was pure bad luck they showed up when someone was home, but with the story you'd given them, they would have killed me trying to get money that didn't exist in the first place. And you called out the ones who were after us last night, too. Again, why? Because you have something to hide. And who else could have known to call out the boys to the scene of the shooting Friday night? And who scared off the Shreiner Agency? Who else could have known to call Brogan and scare him off? Don't try to kid me. You were partners with Wilson for years; you had to know the name of his closest friend. The only reason you didn't scare off his old girlfriend is because you couldn't find her. She'd married and changed her name and moved away.''

''I assume you can prove all this.''

''Not in court, but where I need to, I can.''

''I beg your pardon?''

''You should, for trying to kill me at least twice. I can prove it with a phone call to my contact. He'll know immediately those men weren't following orders from him. He'll know with a couple of phone calls that they took on a job for you.''

He was starting to get his nerve back. ''Assuming for purposes of discussion that I did as you say, that still doesn't connect me with anything they would really care about. If I had the connections to call out people on my own, then why should they care if I used them?''

''It's not just that you use them, but what you use them for. In this case, it shows you were covering up your theft.''

''And what evidence is there of that, except your own speculations years after the fact?''

''Daniel Wilson.''

His brow knitted. ''He's been dead for years. Don't play games with me.''

''He's very much alive.''

''No! I don't believe it.''

''You'd better. If you don't, and he comes forward and tells his story, you'll be sorry. You're in triple trouble; you stole from them, you lied to them about who did it, and you sent out one of their men on a cover-up errand that got him killed.''

''Are you trying to threaten me with criminal charges?''

''Hell, no. I'm not going to fuck around with that. All I have to do is call one of these numbers.'' I handed him the business card, now creased and grimy, with the telephone numbers.

He looked at the card for along time, much longer than it took to understand what it meant. He swallowed and his hand shook. He handed the card back as if trying to force the genie back in the bottle. "What do you want? I think we can reach an accommodation."

"Two hundred and twenty thousand dollars."

"You're insane!"

"And that's not all. Your firm is going to vote to pay off the Wilson estate its one hundred thousand for Wilson's share of the partnership—without the insurance money."

"This—this—"

"And it's going to be done by noon today."

He sat there with his mouth open, trying to absorb it all. "How can I possibly—"

"Put the squeeze on your banker for a fast home equity loan, clean out your accounts, get a cash advance on your bankcard, call your friends, sell your stock, and go to the loan sharks for the rest."

"But they'll charge me a point a day! There's no way I could ever repay—"

I was getting tired of his whining. I pulled out the magnum and placed the muzzle on the bridge of his nose.

"Now pay attention, because I'm only going to say this once. If you don't have the money by noon, I call my contact and tell him what I know. You're dead by evening, and I really don't care. Most of the money is going to the mob to repay what you stole. I hate doing this, but I can't buy peace for one of you without doing it for the other. Personally I'd prefer to see you dead. You may wind up that way anyway; if you don't repay the loan sharks you know what happens. But I'm giving you more of a chance than you ever wanted to give me or Lisa. Or Dan."

"You can't be so arbitrary! You have to give me

some time to work this—'' I leaned close to his face. ''Strasnick, listen up. I had a friend who was an assistant DA. One night the Philly police called him to the scene of where the mob had been questioning one of their people about a theft, just like this one. They'd taken him out to his garage, parked his car on top of his hands, and used his own lawn mower on him. From the cigarette butts, it looked like they'd been there a long time. If you want to go that way it's fine with me.''

He started to sob—strange, choking sounds unlike any human noise I'd ever heard. I put the gun away.

''I want the money in cash—large bills—in a briefcase. It must be ready at noon. The meeting place will be in Center City. I'll call your office later this morning when I know where.'' His sobbing continued. ''Look, tell me right now. Can you do it by noon or should I just go ahead and make the call?''

''No—I can do it.''

He was looking down, his mouth hanging slightly open, looking at something a hundred miles in the ground.

''And one more thing.'' He didn't look up. ''You made quite a speech two days ago about what it means to be partners. Tell me just how you got around to fingering him. I want to know.''

He looked at me mildly. His voice was barely above a whisper. ''Does it matter now?''

''It matters to me.''

''For years we'd busted our asses. Working fourteen-hour days, kissing ass with clients. I hardly ever saw my kids. And we were still broke.

Then they came along. We had it made. Until Dan lost his nerve.''

"Couldn't you just go on without him?''

"With any other client, sure. But if he walked, they'd never trust us again. They're not very trusting people. They don't accept excuses for things like that. The day he left was the last day we'd have all those clients. I had the other lawyers to think of, and my family. . . .'' He looked into my eyes and trailed off.

I got out. I spent a couple of minutes back in Lisa's car, putting the shotgun back on safe, hiding it, and generally pulling myself together. When we drove away, the Mercedes still hadn't moved.

Then they quieted down. We had to run

13

MONDAY, 8:00 A.M.

As I headed toward Philadelphia, the eastern sky was streaked with pink and rose. In my mood it reminded me of blood, but I kept that to myself. We were still too early for the start of the rush hour, but traffic was heavy.

"Lisa, there aren't any assets in Dan's estate other than the hundred-thousand-dollar insurance policy are there?"

She'd finally shaken off the hangover from the sleeping pills. "No. Nothing. Why do you ask?"

"So if the family collected the hundred thousand from another source, walking away from the hearing wouldn't cost anything?"

"That's right, but where would the money come from? I mean, except for the insurance company?"

"What's your share of it?"

"All. Mom has renounced her share in favor of me. I'm the only other heir."

"I have a proposition for you."

"Okay."

"If I could get you the hundred thousand without

going through with the hearing, would you be willing to drop the case?''

"Yes. But how can you do that?''

"I've got a plan. It's still tentative. First I've got some calls to make.''

"What kind of plan?''

"I've got to finish working this out. We'll talk more later.''

When we crawled as far as City Line Avenue I got off and found a pay phone. First, I called Mark Louchs.

"Hello?'' From the sound of his voice I'd woken him up. That made me feel better.

"Mark, this is Dave.''

"Oh! Great. I was wondering what the hell happened. When I hire an investigator I expect him to keep in closer contact.''

Asshole, I thought to myself. "That's a long story. Look, I think the case is going to fold up.''

"What are you talking about?''

"I can't say right now. Just take that on faith, okay?''

"If you say so.''

"I do. But I can't say more now. Things are in a state of flux. I'll know more in an hour or so. Listen, you have this case on an hourly rate or contingent?''

"Hourly.''

"Would a thousand cover your time and expenses to date?''

"Shreiner returned us what we'd paid them, so yes, I think so.''

"If I can make this deal fly, I'll be in a position to guarantee your fee.'' If I didn't I'd be at the bottom of Tinnicum Marsh.

"Fine, thank you. But what's going on?"

"I'll fill you in later." It was the first lie I'd told him. "Have to go now. 'Bye."

Next, I called the bottom number on the card the attorney had given me.

"Yeah?" a male voice answered. Not polite or rude, just neutral.

"This is Dave Garrett. I was told I could reach the counselor at this number."

I was put on hold. The line produced a series of clicks, buzzes, and intermittent tones. Once, it sounded completely dead and I was sure I'd been disconnected. But then his voice, unmistakable, came on the line. It was full and clear and it felt as if he were in the booth with me. I didn't like it.

"Good morning, Mr. Garrett. You're an early riser."

"There have been some developments that you'll be interested in."

"I'm listening."

"I have a proposal that I think you'll like."

"Business should be done face-to-face."

"I agree. That's why I'm calling."

"Where are you now?"

"At the City Line exit off the Schuylkill. In a phone booth."

"Perhaps you are. Wait in your car at your office." The connection was broken.

We headed south on City Line and stopped at a fast-food joint for breakfast. I didn't notice the name of the franchise or what we ordered, but I recall going into the washroom and looking in the mirror. I looked like a panhandler who'd lost a fight over a bottle of Mad Dog. My face was dirty and unshaven, my hair was a mess, and the bruises were ripening to a sickly olive-yellow.

"What's the plan?" Lisa asked when we sat down to eat.

"We're dealing with the big boys. We edged out their second string. And even their first string, once. But our luck is going to run out real soon; we have to end this. The only way to do that is to talk to them. Straighten this out. If this doesn't fly I'm in trouble. If you're with me, you're in trouble, too. Up to now you've just been someone who's with me. They have no reason to get you. To keep it that way you have to stay clear."

"We're in this together."

"Nice thought, but there's nothing you can do to help. All you can do is endanger yourself. So stay out."

"I won't do it. You're in this because of me."

"Lisa, cut it out. You can't help me in this. You can only make it worse."

"What's going on? Why did you want to talk to Strasnick?"

"Even telling you would endanger you. And there isn't time to get into it, anyway. Just take it easy."

She didn't like it, but she didn't argue, either. We ate quickly and headed out. I stopped in front of a branch of the public library about a half mile from my office. I kept my eyes open; no one seemed to be following. "Just go in there and sit tight. I'll be back in an hour or two." If I'm back at all.

"Listen, please take good care of yourself," she said.

"I haven't done very well so far, have I?"

"You're still alive. I want you to stay that way."

"So do I."

"Cut the crap, Dave. You know what I mean."

"When this is all over we're going to have lots to time. Last night meant a lot to me. Now get inside before somebody sees you."

She kissed me on the lips, hard, and I kissed her back. For a moment she pressed her cheek against mine. Then she got out of the car. As she walked away, I saw that her bandage was bloody again. It gave me an unpleasant feeling, half a fear and half a memory. I thought how easy it would be for someone to let all of her life out, not just that little bit of blood, right here on the sidewalk. All they needed was a clean shot and a getaway car. And if I failed it might come to that. I hoped I'd sounded more certain about her own safety than I really felt.

I drove to my office and parked out front. Fortunately for my nerves I didn't have long to wait. Within ten minutes a car with two men I hadn't seen before pulled up. The one in the back motioned for me to get in. The search was conducted in silence. Then we got on Roosevelt Boulevard and headed north. We took an exit in Northeast Philadelphia, cut through a shopping center, and stopped in front of a brick bungalow in a residential area. The driver escorted me to the door. The other man followed us at a safe distance and then headed around to the rear.

The house was barren of any furnishings, and unheated. Still, it was clean. Probably in between tenants. As soon as I shut the door behind me, I heard footsteps upstairs, on the stairway. The sound echoed through the bare rooms. The lawyer appeared, wearing a black hat, yellow silk scarf, and a black cashmere overcoat. He was fresh and rested, and despite his years there was a bounce in his step. Leaning against the door for support, I felt like his grandfather.

"Mr. Garrett." He squinted slightly when my face moved into the light. "What happened?"

"Occupational injuries. From Saturday night."

He nodded slowly. "Saturday night. Accidental?"

"No."

"My client wasn't involved." It was a statement of fact, not just a reassurance. I felt a little better knowing he kept himself so well informed.

"If they were, it wasn't a matter of policy, I'm sure."

"Please come into the kitchen. We have a table and some chairs. It's a crude arrangement, but this is short notice."

We sat down across from each other with our coats on, our breath visible in the air. I liked the cold; it kept me from sweating so much. He studied me for a moment before he spoke.

"You said you had a proposal?"

I moistened my lips and spoke slowly. I couldn't lie and I couldn't give anything away that I didn't have to. "Seven years ago a certain item disappeared. A hundred thousand dollars in cash. A misunderstanding arose as to the identity of the person responsible. What my clients need now is . . . let me choose the right word. Amnesty."

He spoke abruptly. "Are you saying that Wilson wasn't responsible?"

"I'm saying that it was more complex than you were led to believe."

"Answer my question."

There was no point in being indirect. I wasn't going to play games to cover Strasnick. "Yes. A mistake was made."

"How can you be sure?"

"One of my clients told me so."

"Who exactly?"

"I can't say without breaching multiple confidences."

"Please." It wasn't a request.

I temporized. "Once you hear me out you'll see what I mean."

"All right."

"In exchange for amnesty, my clients are prepared to replace the missing property. And as a token of their sincerity, they will pay a one-hundred-percent penalty. Two hundred thousand. Further, the payment will be ready at noon today. The hearing scheduled for today to investigate the Wilson disappearance will be canceled. And the case will be withdrawn permanently."

"So Wilson is alive, somehow."

I swallowed. The thought of actually trying to lie to this man terrified me. "The bullets didn't kill him."

He made an angry gesture at the upstairs. For the first time there was real emotion in his voice. "These men today—cars, bombs, rifles, even! Long range, indirect. They want distance. They don't want to look their man in the eye. The old ways were the best. You knew the job was done. You had to *come to grips*, you understand? They don't like that anymore. But with the old ways there were no mistakes, no loose ends, like now."

I nodded slightly.

"Where is he?"

"I can't say."

We locked eyes while he appraised me. Or rather, while he appraised whether it was worth the trouble to find out where Wilson was. It took no more than five seconds, but in that time I saw what some dead men have seen. He didn't care if he killed me or not, if it advanced the interests of his client. In the house were two or three men who could work me over this morning, kill me, and forget it by dinner; and if he said the word, I was theirs. I thought about the lawn mower.

I leaned closer. "I came here trusting that we could speak in good faith. You told me Saturday that I had your authority to try to help recover the money. I've done that for you, and more. I've doubled your money and caused the Wilson hearing to be dropped. All without any publicity and at no charge to you. If we have a deal, then you don't need to know. Our deal was the return of the property. Not information."

He considered me. Then, very slowly, he relaxed and his eyes clouded over again. He leaned back in the chair and nodded.

"We know what we need to know." He seemed to be talking to himself, his mind on something else. "The property would be in what form?"

"Cash, large bills, in a briefcase."

"And who exactly are you representing? Exactly who is getting forgiveness?" His voice was bored; he knew the answer already.

The rules of confidentiality didn't make much sense under the circumstances. "One of the parties you know already; the Wilson family. The other's identity—well, there's no point in trying to keep it a secret—is Leo Strasnick.''

"I'm a bit surprised that Mr. Strasnick feels he needs his own representation."

"He decided that just this morning."

"And that he feels that his interests are in accord with those of the Wilson family."

"They are. And that is exactly the point of my proposal."

"We may have to reevaluate the utility of a continuing relationship with attorney Strasnick."

"That's up to you, as long as we have a deal."

"Amnesty." He said it slowly, mulling over the word on his tongue.

"For both." It stuck in my throat, but I got it out.

He sighed, and nodded slightly. "Mr. Garrett, the amount of money at stake isn't large. This is an old matter, a file that should be closed. Your terms are acceptable." He was bored, and he spoke rapidly. "My people will pick you up at a place of your choosing in the downtown area with the money at noon. They will take you to a neutral location for the audit and then drop you where you wish. Where shall I have them pick you up?"

"Corner of Sixteenth and Market." Strasnick's building.

"Fine. That concludes our present business." His voice took on a different note; no warmer, but less formal. "Mr. Garrett, you handle yourself well. Have you had a chance to consider my offer of a referral to new counsel on your reinstatement?"

"Thank you, I have. But the answer is still no."

"No?"

I thought about the best way of phrasing it. "It would be a debt I would have trouble repaying."

He nodded absently, another matter closed. "The audit will be handled by one of my assistants. We will not be meeting again. And I would trouble you for the return of my card."

"Certainly."

He extended his hand and I took it. The room was cold, but his hand was colder. I hoped I would never have to touch or even see that man again.

Within thirty minutes I was back at the library. She was sitting in the entryway nursing a cup of coffee. When she looked up, she looked behind me to see if I was alone. "How are we doing?"

"Everything's fine. We shook hands on the deal. It will all be over by noon."

"Can you tell me what's going on now?" She was sounding exasperated and I couldn't blame her.

"If there's a problem at the other end, with Strasnick, there could still be trouble. I can't say any more than that. Come on."

We got into her car and headed south, with no destination in particular. I was more concerned than I let on with Lisa. I had to kill two hours and I felt safer on the move in a big city than in a fixed location. Not that I was expecting any trouble in particular, but I'd already had a bellyful of the unexpected kind.

"Lisa, we need to have a talk."

"We sure do. Can you tell me what's going on now?"

"We need to talk about the past before we talk about the present."

"What are you talking about?"

"You know what."

"No, I don't."

"The whole thing started seven years ago with a hundred thousand in cash that belonged to the mob. Strasnick took it and blamed in on Dan. That's why they were after him. That's what Strasnick and I talked about in the car. He's going to replace the money, with interest."

"Strasnick?"

"He knew I could prove that he'd been after me, but he really didn't care about that. His friends in the organization wouldn't care if he had a grudge against an outsider, if that was all there was to it. He was only worried about the money being traced back to him. He didn't believe I had any proof about what happened seven years ago."

She said nothing.

"What do you think I told him?"

"I don't know." Her voice was very soft.

"Yes, you do."

Silence.

I did something I'd never done, either as a lawyer or investigator: I begged a witness. "Lisa, don't make me do this."

She didn't answer.

"I'd like you to tell me yourself."

Silence. I was busy driving and couldn't look at her.

"Lisa, I told him Daniel Wilson is alive."

I pulled over and parked.

14

MONDAY, 10:00 A.M.

She looked out the window a long time without speaking, so long I thought she hadn't heard. I was about to say something when I caught a glimpse of the side of her face. I can't describe what I saw, except to say that it was something that needed to be let alone.

"It's not an easy thing to talk about," she said at last.

"I can imagine."

"No, not like that. I'm not embarrassed. It's—like, for seven years I've been able to pretend that I've always been this way, that it's never been any different. That everything else in my life never happened."

I waited.

"Did you ever want something you couldn't have?" She was facing away from me and her voice was muffled.

"Sure."

"I mean, not a thing. But something you wanted to be, that you couldn't be." When I hesitated, she went on. "Like you wanted to be somebody, to do something, and then found you couldn't."

"I don't know. When I was in college I wanted to be a doctor."

"Did you want it real bad?"

"Yeah." I thought of saying more, and decided that I could either talk for an hour or leave it right there. "Yeah."

"And what happened?"

"I couldn't get into medical school. I was trying in the years when it was the worst as far as getting in. Unless you had straight A's there was no chance. So I went to law school instead."

"Imagine something more important, a hundred times more important than just what you do for a living. Something you can't ever decide to quit and do something else instead. And imagine you think about it every day of your life from your first memories. That's what it's like."

She turned away from the window and looked at her hands in her lap. "When I think of my childhood, all I can think of are my sister and my mother. Dad was never around. When he wasn't working he stayed away from home a lot. He and Mom hated each other. And even when he was home, he stayed inside his shell. Never talking to anyone, just reading the paper or watching TV and biding his time till he could get out of there again. When he died I was sad, but it didn't change anything."

She smiled sadly and played with a small ring on her right little finger. "I don't blame him. It's no one's fault. It just *is*. But anyway, Lisa and I played together all the time; we were always close.

When I was a baby she and Mom would dress me up in Lisa's baby things and she'd use me as a doll. When I got a little older, maybe two or three, they started dressing me in the clothes she'd outgrown. I know it seems so strange, but it didn't then. I didn't understand about boys and girls; all I knew was that Lisa was my sister and we did everything together. And we were happy. From my earliest memories I associated playing with Lisa, just us two girls, with being happy.''

"Lisa, you don't have to tell me all of this if you don't want to."

For the first time she looked at me, and there was anger in her eyes. The fact that it wasn't directed at me didn't make it any easier. "Damn it, besides my doctor and my mother, you're the only person in the whole world who knows or who will *ever* know. And you're not going to get out of this car thinking I'm some kind of pervert or sickie or something."

"Okay."

"Do you know anything about this kind of thing?"

"No."

"Then you start with the two-minute program on nomenclature. There're three reasons why a man would wear women's clothes, and they're all completely different. Most common is homosexuals. Some gay men like to wear women's things—well, for the same reason women do, to attract men. Just like gays, or straights even, dress up in leather. It's a costume thing. Then there are transvestites, straight men who are turned on by women's clothes. They like women, and just like most women they like seeing women in sexy clothes. But they like wearing the clothes themselves, too. And then there's the rarest type of all, the transsexual. A man who doesn't wear women's clothes to attract gay men—because he isn't gay. He doesn't wear them because they sexually excite him. He does it because it seems right to do it. Because he thinks he's really a woman.''

She cleared her throat and went on. ''The first time I really learned anything was wrong was when I went to school. Mom bought me some brand-new scratchy jeans and said I would have to wear them from now on. I hated them. I hated the boys being separated from the girls and having to stay with the boys. Lisa let me wear her underpants to school, under my jeans. And it made me feel better. Like, I may have to dress like this on the outside, but I can be me underneath. And Mom knew about it; she must have. She did the wash. She never said anything to either one of us. At home I still shared clothes with Lisa. But I knew that people outside the family weren't supposed to know about that. So I learned to be ashamed, but I didn't understand why.

''Things got pretty bad when I got to be a teenager. I started growing, my voice changed. I never had much hair on my chest or arms, but the little I had, I hated. I found myself changing into something strange. I used to think that if I avoided certain foods I could stop it, like they were poisoning me and making my body do these things. And with gym, I had to learn to be more careful about my underclothes. Once I got caught and beaten up. They said I was a fairy; I didn't even know what

they were talking about. Anyway, Lisa was older
and she let me share her things—bras and slips and
stockings. I'd wear them on the days I didn't have
gym, and at home. And it felt so good; it was me.
Putting on male clothes, I felt like one of those
medieval knights putting on armor—it was ugly and
clunky and uncomfortable, but it was something
you had to do to protect yourself from the world.
The only good thing about dressing like a man was
how good it felt to get the clothes off again.''

"It must have been complicated."

"You don't know the half. Around sixteen, I
started cross-dressing completely, and going out in
public. Lisa taught me about makeup, and I bought
a wig. At first I'd just go out with Lisa for a drive.
Then I'd go for walks late at night by myself. I was
careful not to walk around our own neighborhood.
Then Lisa and I started going shopping; that was
fun, especially buying clothes. The more I went
out dressed up, the more comfortable I became.
And the better I got at it. There are a million little
things that men and women do differently. And I
don't mean the obvious ones, like the pitch of your
voice. It's how you sit, how you walk, the way you
hold your elbows, gesturing. Plus the makeup has
to be just right to hide the beard.''

She smiled again. "Let me tell you, the walking
part is *hard*. Women's hips don't go from side to
side because they decide to do it. It's natural. Their
hips are wider and the whole center of gravity when
they walk is a little different. I had to work at it.
But by the time I was out of college, I could pass
in any situation. At one point I even took a part-
time job as a salesclerk as a woman. It was a good

time. I had a circle of friends, strictly off-campus people, who knew me only as a woman.''

"What did Lisa think?''

"She accepted me. Sometimes she said she was sorry for me, that my life had become so complicated, but we joked about it, too. Sometimes someone would call for Danny and I'd be dressed up as a woman, ready to go out, and I'd be talking on the phone about the Flyers or something in my masculine voice. Then the next night someone would call for Danielle—that was the name I used then—when I was in man's clothes and I'd have to use my feminine voice. It always cracked her up. But mainly, she understood.''

"What about your mom?''

"We never really discussed it. She'd see me coming and going, sometimes dressed as a man, sometimes as a woman. She never said anything to me dressed one way that she wouldn't have said otherwise. Well, not quite. Once she told me not to wear high heels because it was icy.''

"When you were in practice, you were cross-dressing then, and you had a blond wig.''

"How did you—'' she started, then stopped. "Someone saw me.''

"Harrison, the black fellow from across the street. He was fooled. Strasnick said you lived very simply.''

"Some of my money I saved. I traveled with the rest. When I was out of town, I could live as a woman without having to look over my shoulder.''

"There must have been times when you resented your mother and sister. For playing a part in the whole situation. Allowing it to develop.''

She looked at the ceiling of the car. "That, David, is the sixty-four-thousand-dollar question. I spent years in counseling, and that's the one way it helped."

"Go on. If you want to."

"You don't know how much I do. When you have a problem like mine, you go through phases. Sometimes you accept yourself and sometimes you think you're really a sick person. When I first started cross-dressing and going out, I used to feel very conflicted. That's a good psychological term for it. I'd feel great in a way, that the real me was getting out; and I'd feel like a jerk, too. There were times I hated myself as much as any ignorant fagbasher could have. When I was in that kind of a mood, I really hated them both."

"Did you ever confront them?"

"The moods didn't last long, and they stopped after a while. Later I came to see that they were like growing pains; it was a rearguard action that my masculine personality was fighting as the feminine side took over. I don't know if that makes any sense to you. It's hard for anyone else to understand."

"It's all new to me."

"Thanks. At least you're not being condescending."

"You were explaining about your mom and your sister."

"I got sidetracked. What counseling showed me was that I had to make a basic choice about how I was going to see myself. If I was no good, a loser, a freak, then I ought to hate myself and blame my family. But if I felt good about myself, there was nobody to blame. It's a matter of accepting yourself.''

"That part must have been hard.''

"At fifteen, or twenty, I couldn't have done it. Accepting your limitations is never easy, no matter what they are or how old you are.''

"It's a lot to accept, for you.''

"I'm not going to tell you that if I'd had the choice I would have wanted it this way. I used to think, why couldn't I just have been a normal guy? But that's thinking like a victim—'Why did it have to be me that got cancer?' I'm past that. And in one way, I was lucky.''

"Go on.''

"I was fairly short for a man, with a thin build, not very muscular. I could make the change and be convincing. What if I'd been six-five and two hundred fifty pounds?''

"Want to know what I'm thinking?''

"Sure.''

"On Saturday morning, in my office, you complimented me for being a strong person because I accepted responsibility for cheating on the bar exam. I've got no right to take compliments from you. That's peanuts compared to this.''

"Thank you. But you see, it's what you have to do. One of my counselors told me, when I was having a bad day, that I ought to go complain to the person who issued me a warranty at birth, guaranteeing that I'd live to be eighty, in perfect health, with no problems. That helped me decide I had to make the best of it.''

"Did Leo Strasnick know?''

"God, no. No one outside the family knew. And now there's just Mom."

"Did you ever try to tell anyone?"

"Oh, sure. More when I was younger. I was dumber then. I thought people just might be understanding, or at least tolerant. It would always go the same way; I'd start out with a remark about cross-dressing, something neutral. The response was always how they couldn't believe anyone could be sick enough to do something like that. I'd say something more, they'd talk about how the goddamn queers were taking over and molesting kids. Then I'd give up."

"You never told Elizabeth."

"If there's anything in my life I really regret, that was it."

"Regret?"

"I was using her and she didn't know it."

"I've met her. There was plenty of that coming from the other direction."

"I started seeing her on my counselor's recommendation. He said that before I took an irrevocable step I should try once more."

"Let me guess. He told you that going out with a woman a little on the aggressive side might help."

"Actually, no; it just turned out that way. For a while it was okay. There was nothing wrong with her as a person, and I was lonely. But once we started having sex, I knew it wasn't going to work. There was nothing wrong with her physically, and I liked her well enough; I just didn't want to do it. I had to force myself. I realized once and for all, that I wasn't attracted to women any more than any other straight woman would be."

"You started ducking her by going out of town on weekends again."

"You know what I told my counselor? It came out purely by accident. 'It's such a relief to get out of town and be myself.' That's when I knew there was no turning back."

"You'd been saving for a sex change operation?"

An edge of bitterness crept in. "Yes, at first. By the way, the proper term is sex reassignment. After three years I thought I might have enough saved, so I went to Johns Hopkins. Lots of fees, lots of forms, interviews, psychological assessments, personality profiles, MMPIs, medical exams, blood studies."

"What happened?"

"Nothing. They told me to get counseling to help myself adjust to being a man. I said I'd done that in college, for two years. But sexual orientation isn't something you think through; you just have it. If our society decided tomorrow that homosexuality was normal, and that liking women was a sickness you should be cured of, how much would counseling help you adjust to that?" I said nothing. "Anyway, they said to go and get some more. They told me I wasn't a good candidate for surgery anyway. Ready for this? I was too normal. Stable personality, no delusions, not suicidal, coping adequately with society. They told me I didn't need it."

We both let the silence stretch out, letting it all settle. "I guess the only other thing is to tell me what really happened."

"You were right about everything between Strasnick and me. He took the money; he said he'd be putting it right back. For the good of the firm, he said. I was concerned, but I had no idea they were really after me. I thought if I pulled out of the firm I could put everything with the mob behind me. I was about to give Strasnick my formal notice of withdrawal and get a fresh start. I'd even drawn my money out of the bank. I'd made up my mind to have the operation, even if I had to go out of the country. Lisa was in town; we talked about the operation. She was very supportive—she knew how long I'd been thinking about it. My plan was to live with Lisa in LA for a few months as a woman, take hormone treatments, and then have the surgery. I was going to use the time to think about what I was going to do next. Whatever it was going to be, it wasn't going to be working for the mob any longer. Anyway, they must have followed us all day, like you said, waiting to catch us alone.''

''You were cross-dressed.''

''Uh-huh. Come to think of it, I don't know what they would have thought of that—maybe they assumed it was a disguise. I guess they thought if I had really stolen the money, I would try to disguise myself. If they started following me from my apartment, following my car, they had to know it was me. Anyway, I was driving north on Ten when a car pulled alongside; but it didn't pass. The passenger started shooting. The rest is just like I told you, except Lisa was the one who was slow in ducking, not me. I'm sure she never felt a thing.''

''You got to a phone, called your mom, and called it in.''

''Yes, but I didn't call the police until after Mom had arrived and we'd talked about it. She got there two hours later and we went back to the car.''

"By that time you had a plan."

She nodded. "It sounds so cold-blooded now. But I was still in shock; my mind was working but I was all numb inside. And I knew that nothing— could bring Lisa back."

"You went back to the car and moved the body."

"I thought of putting her in the trunk, but it was too risky. So I hid her in some woods."

"Then you drove to the police station in your mom's car. Where was your mother, by the way?"

"At the McDonald's at the Morgantown exit. There was no way to explain her being up there."

"And you gave your statement in the car instead of inside because you were afraid you'd be detected."

"I stopped at a convenience store and bought a razor and some shaving cream. I cleaned up as best I could at the McDonald's. I stripped off my makeup, shaved, and put on fresh. I tried hard to comb all the glass out of my wig. I knew I'd be a suspect. They'd look at me as closely as they could. But Dietz was basically a pretty nice guy about it, and God knows I didn't have to fake being upset."

"And then?"

"It was time to say good-bye to Lisa." She put her head down again, but didn't sob. All of the tears had been cried a long time ago. "Mom and I had talked about it. If they thought I was dead I'd be safe. If they knew they'd killed the wrong person they'd be back. So I would take over her identity. We couldn't let the body be found, of course. I had her wrapped in a blanket. There's a huge abandoned quarry, I think it was for limestone, for a steel company, a few miles west. I knew about it because the gatehouse had been used as a drug drop by some of my clients. The quarry was flooded to the top; the water must have been a hundred feet deep. I wrapped her up as carefully as I could and said good-bye. That's where she is.''

"It must have been very hard."

"If I'd had time to really think about it, I couldn't have done it. But there was no other way. And—I don't know if there's an afterlife or not, but if there is, she knows how we felt about her.''

"She would have wanted you to do it.''

"Thank you. I like to think so.''

"Not just hiding her; I mean, pretending to be her. What happened to her gave you your chance.''

She nodded. ''The next thing was the operation. There's a clinic on an island in the Caribbean, Curaçao, that does them purely on demand; no screening or waiting. I'd thought of going to them after Johns Hopkins turned me down, but I hadn't been sure before. I was scared of winding up with some butcher who didn't even speak English. But they were very good. The problem was me, not them. Most patients come in after months or years of hormone therapy. I came in cold. And I needed a lot of depilation in a hurry.''

"Depilation?''

"Hair removal. The hormones help, but the facial hair and some of the other body hair has to come off by electrolysis. It hurts when you do a lot at a time; I would sit through two sessions a day, as much as I could stand. It hurt more than the surgery, and that hurt a lot, especially when I started moving around. They did breast implants; they said they were guessing about the positioning because the hormones would change my body shape. They came out a little bigger than I wanted. I also had them cut down my Adam's apple. There's a word for the operation but I forget. Later on I had a nose job. It's funny; my nose was fine when I was a man, but after the hormones took hold it was too big.''

"The hormones were to help your breasts grow?''

"It does a lot more than that. It makes your skin soft; it eliminates most of your body hair and changes the distribution of what's left; it changes around the fat distribution. Men carry their extra weight in their abdomens; women carry it in the thighs and hips. It changes your voice. But the main thing it changes is your personality.''

"I don't understand.''

"How you cope with stress. A man's testosterone is always pushing him, making him aggressive, wanting to fight. You take that away, and you can think so clearly. It's like you've spent your whole life with someone shouting in your ear, urging you to pick fights, and then they shut up. The silence is wonderful. If something goes wrong now, I may cry a bit, but then I pull myself together and solve the problem. I don't feel any urge to grit my teeth and start World War Three. Want to hear a story?''

"Sure.''

"After the operation, after all the treatments, when everything was done, I would go to Common Pleas in Philly and watch my old friends try cases. No one ever recognized me. And watching them was a hoot. There'd be a simple case, so easy to settle, but one or the other—or both—of the guys would want to prove how tough he was. They would rationalize all day about why this or that principle was important, or why it had to be tried. But what it really came down to was, they were all being led around by their balls. The testosterone said, 'Fight,' and they fought. They're just cavemen with briefcases; there's really been no progress in a million years. 'What do you mean, settle? I can try this! I'm hard! I'm ready! I'll show you!' '' She laughed. ''I don't mean to go on and on, but it's such a relief being able to talk to someone.''

''Go ahead, if you want.''

''The doctors wanted me to stay in Curaçaco for two weeks. But that would have made the police suspicious. They wanted to reinterview me. Mom was running out of excuses. So I gritted my teeth and came back in five days. The hormones hadn't taken hold and the depilation wasn't a hundred percent complete, but I knew I could pass. I took some pain medication and got through it.''

''I know this is a hell of a question, but any regrets?''

She laughed. ''Only when I have to look for a public restroom.'' Her smile faded a little and she leaned back in the seat. She closed her eyes. ''Let me tell you about my flight back. I was traveling on Dan Wilson's passport of course. Lisa didn't have one; and even if she had, we didn't look enough alike that I could have used her photo. So I went down dressed as a man, and coming back I had to dress as a man. I hid my breasts by bandaging them flat and wearing a floppy tropical shirt. The plane changes got screwed up and I was in transit almost fifteen hours. It was stinking hot when I cleared customs in Philly. It was the middle of the night. My incisions were still draining and I was so tired I could barely see straight. I was air-sick, and my face was raw from depilation. I found an empty women's restroom, took in my suitcase, took off my male clothes and threw them in the garbage. I unbandaged my breasts and put on a bra and panties and a summer dress. I tried to put on a little lipstick, but I couldn't—I was so happy I was sobbing uncontrollably. As hot and tired and sick as I was. It had all been a bad dream and finally it was over. That was how good it felt to finally be me after thirty years of living a lie. And that's the way I feel this minute.''

We were both quiet for a time after that. Then I looked at my watch; it was time to talk business again.

''You couldn't practice law and you certainly couldn't be a scrub nurse, so you took this job.''

''Earning money wasn't important. I had enough to pay cash for the house, even after the surgery and the travel. Living up there helped me keep a low profile as far as the mob was concerned. Plus I had to stay clear of anyone who knew Lisa. When I went out to Los Angeles to ship her things back and close up her apartment, I didn't try to fake it. I told her neighbors I was her cousin.''

''That's why there are no old pictures of either one of you.''

She nodded. ''Mom and I had to throw away a lot of things. I didn't dare keep anything, of mine or Lisa's, that could give it away. We never knew when someone might check up on me. That's why I brought back all her Spanish-style furniture. And why I faked some old photographs of myself as Lisa.''

''You did a thorough job.''

''The toughest one was the graduation photo from nursing school. I had to make it good enough for people to recognize me and accept it as legitimate. But remember, it's supposed to be a picture of a girl of about twenty-two. I was a good ten years older at that point.''

''If that was the only thing, it would have fooled me.''

''I kept my hormone pills with me so you wouldn't see them if you found an excuse to come nosing around. And I threw away my glasses and got contacts that made my eyes darker.''

''You covered every angle you could.''

''Then it was something about my body.''

''There's nothing wrong with your body. As far as I can recall, you're the best lover I've ever had.''

She dropped her eyes. ''I don't really like asking questions like this. But people like me are very sensitive about passing unnoticed. Thank you for the compliment. Now tell me, how did you know?''

''Sometimes when the facts don't fit the theory you have to bend the facts.''

She just looked at me, waiting.

''First it looked like a disappearance. But then when I saw the mob was involved, I changed my mind. I didn't have a reason why they'd be in this, but that didn't bother me. The only funny thing was the disappearance of Daniel's body. Why hide a body? The mob wouldn't have done it; they want people to know that they kill people who cross them. So someone else hid it. Again, who? Which gets you to why. I was stuck until you admitted you'd been in the same car. Then I knew the killers could have hit the wrong person; you said so yourself. So there's the why—hide the body to conceal the fact that the body isn't that of the intended victim. To protect the victim.''

"That takes you as far as Lisa is dead and Daniel might be still alive, somewhere. It doesn't tell you that I was Daniel.''

"No, but someone fooled Dietz by appearing to be Lisa. Your mom could never have pulled it off; she's too old. On such short notice, it had to be you.''

"Okay, it shows I masqueraded one time, nothing more.''

I shook my head. "If you had to do it once, it meant that you had to follow through or the whole thing would come out. Once you'd decided to play it that Lisa was alive and Dan was dead, you couldn't very well have Dan reappear. I couldn't know about your background or that you'd go as far as an operation, but I knew there was something wrong with Lisa's story even before I figured out that the wrong person was shot. Why would a single young woman with a career go from Los Angeles to coal country?''

"To be closer to home?''

"Home is Philly. The better part of three hours away. And why not get another job in nursing? There are lots of opportunities, especially in a rural area. Because you couldn't.''

"So you suspected before you went to my house.''

"Saying that gives me a hell of a lot more credit than I'm entitled to. Let's just say I was puzzled."

"What did you find that convinced you?"

"I wasn't convinced even then. Maybe a little more puzzled. But to answer your question, it was what I didn't find. Like no tampons. And how many people of any means don't have at least some childhood pictures of themselves and their family? Not one shot of Dan and Lisa together, even considering that you'd been so close. You cleaned house *too* thoroughly."

"I went to a lot of trouble to fake the pictures that were there."

"The pictures that you did have around the place threw me for a while. Everything nicely documented. But when I thought about it later, I wasn't so sure. It looked too pat. Especially after I found out how much Dan was into photography."

"How did you know about that?"

"Elizabeth. And the guy across the street from your old apartment. And your photography club in college."

"It's a common thing among people with a—gender problem. I used to take lots of pictures of myself cross-dressed. To reassure myself, somehow. It's hard to explain. But after the surgery there was no need."

"You cleaned house with Lisa's friends, too. Not everybody has a million friends, but not to see any of your old friends in seven years?"

"But none of that is enough. Tell me; there has to be something about my body."

"No. It was a lot simpler than that. It's easier to hide your sex than who you are as a person. It was how you acted. Little things, like when we met the first day, you initiated shaking hands a couple of times. Women don't do that very often. You were careful to choose your words, but every so often you'd use a word that wouldn't come naturally to a nurse. When we were at your mom's apartment you talked about a 'limited purpose.' ''

"Anyone could say that."

"Sure, but we both know it's a term of art in evidence law. It's something Dan would have known. At your house you said 'burden of proof.' And in the car you talked about 'perjuring' yourself."

"And I thought I was doing such a good job of playing dumb with all my questions about law."

"There was more to it than that. You didn't know things any experienced nurse would know. You didn't seem concerned about whether I had a concussion. You talked about 'stitches' instead of 'sutures,' and you took my pulse the wrong way. You put your thumb on my wrist, not your first two fingers. The thumb has a pulse of its own, so you should keep the thumb away from the inside of the wrist. Anyone with any nursing training would know not to take a pulse that way. But except for that you faked it pretty nicely. If I hadn't been hurt I might never have made the connection."

"So last night—"

"No, I didn't know then. I still thought you were hiding him. I hadn't made the leap yet. Want to know what really gave it away? Something really simple, once I thought about it. When I was at Elizabeth's house she showed me a letter Dan wrote to her. The handwriting looked familiar. I figured there must have been a sample of Dan's handwriting in the file. But when I thought back, there wasn't. It looked familiar because I saw your handwriting on that questionnaire you filled out in my office.''

''You're good.''

''No. I'm an idiot. I can't see things at the end of my nose. I had the key to solving the case right in my hand Saturday afternoon. It took me until Monday morning to appreciate it. I just didn't see it.''

She looked away, out the window. Her voice was soft and very sad. ''I'm glad you didn't realize it then. I'm glad we had last night.''

I started the car and watched the gauges to avoid looking at her face. ''It's almost time.''

For the moment there was nothing more that had to be said. We rode without talking; I think both of us were grateful for the silence. I dropped Lisa at my office and headed for Strasnick's office.

15

MONDAY, 11:00 A.M.

The same fashion model was at the reception desk, but this time she was wearing a drop-dead black dress with a gold pin. There wasn't much time to look; she had hardly finished announcing me before Strasnick burst in and hustled me into a small conference room. He was wearing the same jacket, still without a tie. His complexion was terrible—white and blotchy at the same time. His hair was a mess and his eyes were bloodshot. He looked almost as bad as I did. We sat across from each other at a small table inlaid with at least four kinds of wood, plus gold leaf. Even if it was a reproduction, it must have cost more than all the furniture in my apartment. I didn't want to think what it was worth if it was an antique.

Strasnick leaned forward, trying to keep his voice low but not quite succeeding. "We have a problem. There's—"

"What do you mean, 'we'?"

"Cut me a break, Garrett."

"Like you cut your partner?"

"The money's all here. Look." He picked up a

briefcase from the corner and pushed it across the table at me. I opened it. Money bulged out, in every denomination and description: bundles of brand-new five-hundred-dollar bills, still in wrappers; rolls of hundreds wrapped with rubber bands; and handfuls of fifties and twenties lying loose. "It's all there," he repeated eagerly. "Go ahead, count it."

"I'm going to. These people aren't going to take being shorted." I started to count. "Now, what's the problem?"

"My firm. We had an emergency partner's meeting an hour ago. They won't go along with paying off Wilson's estate. And they won't even let me borrow against my equity."

I let him it sit till I'd counted all the five-hundred-dollar balls and put them in a stack to my left. "Then you're going to have to raise the hundred thousand yourself, too."

"You can't mean that. A third of what's here comes from the sharks already. I'm going to need to give them a grand a day just to pay the interest on this."

I rummaged through the case, segregated the hundreds, and counted them out. There were quite a few of them. "Ever occur to you that all of this started with money that wasn't yours to begin with? I mean, if you put a hundred grand in the bank for seven years, it turns into two hundred. All you're doing here is giving back what you stole, with a fee to me for saving your ass. You got off real cheap."

His mouth trembled and I could see his hands

shaking. "This is *it,* Dave. I did everything you said and more. There isn't another nickel!"

The counting slowed down even more on the loose fifties and twenties, but when I was done, the count was exact. I didn't look up at him once. The money was in neat piles all across the table. I took twenty thousand in five-hundred-dollar bills for myself and to pay Louch's fee and marked them with a large paper clip. Then everything went back into the case. It was twenty after eleven.

"This thing's a package; the two-twenty and the hundred. I'll tell you what I'll do, Strasnick. I'm going to give you thirty days to come up with the hundred. If I don't have it I'm going back to the counselor with you." He had no way to know if I was bluffing.

Sweat broke out on his forehead. "I told you—I can't do any more. I'm leveraged like crazy. I was, even before I had to come up with this."

"In thirty days you can sell your house if you knock the price down enough. That place has got to be worth the better part of a million."

"But—I—"

"Take a hundred off the market price, hundred and a quarter. If you can't get to settlement within thirty days, the broker will buy it from you and hold it for resale."

"With the loans against it here's two hundred in equity, tops! I'd sell it and have nothing."

"Listen up. Let me tell you what it means to have a partner, 'cause you don't know. If you can't stand your partner either you dump him or he dumps you. But as long as you're together, you play it straight with him. Absolutely straight. You can cheat on your wife and bullshit the judge and stay drunk every minute you're not working, and it's your own business. But when it comes to your partner, you go hungry instead of hitting the petty cash for lunch money if that isn't part of your deal. Because no matter what else goes on, you have to be able to count on each other. But you—you did worse than leave him alone. You sent them out after him and left him to die. I'd love to give you right back to them. I'll tell you, I'm sorry I even have to give you a chance. It's more than you deserve.''

He looked into my eyes, begging. If he was looking for pity, there was none to be found.

"You can't leave me with nothing. I'm almost forty. I've got a wife and two kids. I can't start from scratch at my age.''

I leaned closer, till I could smell him. I took my time answering. "I leave you with your life.''

He pulled back from me, folding his arms across his chest and hunching over as if he were trying to roll himself into a ball. He closed his mouth tightly and looked down at the table. For a long time he didn't say anything.

"Okay," he whispered at last. "You'll have it.''

I picked up the briefcase and opened the door. He was still in his chair, his head bent. I don't know if he knew I was still there. There was something dead in his eyes.

I put my hand on the knob. I wanted to leave, to put as much distance between myself and Strasnick as I could. But I couldn't just walk out, like a delivery boy on an errand. What Strasnick had done, what had happened in that room, what was in that briefcase, was important. It deserved a moment of its own. One person had been killed and another forced into hiding because of what I was carrying. Now another life was in shambles. Three live had been changed forever by the money. The case felt heavier in my hand.

I looked back at him. "It's over," I whispered. He turned his head, but his eyes looked through me. "It's been a long time, but it's finally over. All your work, your practice, your clients, everything you've built up is gone. It might as well have never happened. You're right back where you started. And you know something? You're the lucky one."

He focused on me briefly, then his eyes glazed over. Down the corridor I could hear a female voice laughing softly. The sound might as well have come from Mars; there was nothing to smile about where I was. My world was about wasted lives and trying to patch them up as best I could.

I could have talked to Strasnick for an hour, but I was the only one listening, anyway. I shut the door behind me without another word.

The rest of the deal went down like clockwork. My ride whisked me to an abandoned warehouse in Camden where the money was counted out by three men in total silence. I pocketed my twenty thousand and met Lisa back at my office. She was sitting where she'd sat for our initial interview a hundred years ago. She stood up like she wanted to throw her arms around me, then stopped. We looked at each other awkwardly.

"It's good to see you again," she said.

"I'm glad it's over."

"I hope that now you can at least tell me exactly what the rest of the deal is."

I was glad of the chance to talk business. "From your point of view it's simple enough. I bought amnesty for you and Strasnick. Or rather, Strasnick did, for both of you. He returned the hundred plus another hundred as a penalty. Plus he paid my fee, and your attorney's fee. And Strasnick will be honoring the buyout provision, so you'll be getting the hundred thousand. In a month."

"They won't be after me?"

"No. That was part of the deal."

"Do they know I'm alive?"

"I didn't tell them in so many words, but they figure you are. Otherwise, why would I propose the deal at all? But they didn't press me on it. You're in the clear with them."

"The hearing is off?"

"Permanently. Part of the deal. I have to call Mark and tell him it's definitely off. And I should probably send a bill to the life insurance company. I did a hell of a day's work for them."

"And me. Thank you. And thanks for listening to my rant."

"Sure. Do you know what you'll be doing now?"

"Two weeks in Cancun. I've been dreading this hearing for a long time. I promised myself a big treat when it was out of the way.'

"No, after that."

"Haven't decided at all. I'll be making some decisions while I'm on the trip, I guess."

"You know, with the organization off you, there's no reason why you can't practice law again."

"Are you serious?"

"Not as Dan Wilson, of course. But Danielle

sounds fine. Or any name. You could even use Lisa, I guess. You can get a change-of-name hearing done discreetly for a couple of hundred bucks. No judge can say that you should be required to go through life as 'Dan' now. Get your name on your license changed and roll.''

''If I don't have to hide who I am—Jesus, you're right. But what kind of a firm could I get into? I can't explain the last seven years. Or why I can't give them references for the five years before that.''

''Forget the firm route. Hang out your own shingle. You'll have a hundred grand as seed money. And you'd be a hell of a family law practitioner. Or a criminal lawyer, if you can get the men to trust a woman. Or whatever you want to be.''

''I'd have a million problems with the police and the bar association. But you're giving me a lot to think about.''

''Let me give you some more. Lisa's dead, but you're the one who's been buried. You've wasted some of the best years of your life in that little town. Until now you could kid yourself that you had to hide out. That excuse is gone now. You've done enough penance. It wasn't your fault.''

We were quiet for a moment, trying to set a rhythm now that our business was done. Then she looked up. ''I need to get you back to your car. And I need to see my doctor about this arm. Can we take a little side trip on the way?''

16

MONDAY, 3:00 P.M.

The gravel road was in poor shape, and my side complained at every jolt. The underside of the car brushed over weeds, brushes, and even some saplings. Numerous rivulets crossed the road, washing away what little gravel remained. At the rate it was eroding, it would be hard to find the road at all in a few more years. With a few inches of snow, it would be invisible even now.

About half a mile after we turned off the last paved road, we came to the rusting, twisted remains of a sign: BETHL—the rest was illegible. A few fifty-five-gallon oil drums, equally rusty, were scattered about. Farther up, we came to a half-collapsed shack. The windows were broken out and the door was missing. A PRIVATE PROPERTY—KEEP OUT sign hung at a crazy angle, shot full of holes.

Lisa pulled behind the shed and parked. "Want to come along?"

"I'd like to, if it's okay with you."

She opened the trunk and pulled out the floral wreath we'd bought at the florist in King of Prussia. It was big, almost four feet in diameter, and she

was having trouble with it in the wind. I stood aside
and tried to break the wind a bit; I was in no position to help further.

The ground ahead was open, except for some
brush and saplings. The day had clouded up and
turned colder since noon. The wind, gusting at unpredictable intervals, made a mess of my attempts
at balance. I stayed on her windward side and concentrated on my feet.

"Here we are."

In front of me was a wide expanse of dark water,
big as a lake, ringed by gray stone cliffs on all
sides. The far side was at least a quarter of a mile
away. The wind was brisk, but the water, sheltered
by the shoreline, was blank and unruffled. As still
and dark as death itself.

"I used to come here a lot," she said after a
while. "Not so often anymore. I'm not sure why I
come. I don't believe in a hereafter; I don't think
she knows we're here. Maybe it's just easier for me
to focus my thoughts here."

"I think it's better than a cemetery."

"Oh?"

"Cemeteries are full of grass and flowers and
inscriptions to cheer up the living. They're pretti-
fied and phony. This is what it should be; it's a
dead place. A place for the dead."

"Funny you should say that," she said. "It's always reminded me of the river Styx, from mythol-
ogy."

She looked out again at the water. The wind
stung our eyes. "Ready?"

"If you are."

She prepared to throw it herself, but I stopped her. "No, let me do this with you."

"But your side."

"I'll use my left arm."

Together we threw the wreath over the edge. My side burned for a moment but I paid no attention. The wreath bounced once on the cliff below us, then rebounded out into the water.

We both stood there watching. Neither of us were believers, or thought we could commune with the dead, so we were left with thinking about the living.

"Did you know that Strasnick was behind this?" I asked. "Back then, I mean."

"I knew he'd kept the money, and that it put us both in trouble. But I never knew he turned me in. All these years I was blaming him just for being greedy and stupid. I never thought that he wanted me dead."

"The loan sharks are going to eat him alive."

"I'm satisfied, if that's what you mean. No matter what you did it wouldn't bring her back."

"You must miss her a lot."

She looked out again over the water, saying nothing. The wreath slowly sank out of sight, on its way to join Lisa on the dark and rocky bottom.

When it disappeared completely she turned to me. "So what about you, once I get you back to your car?"

"I'm not going to be taking on any new cases for a month or so in my condition. And all my bills are paid for a while. I was thinking of a vacation." I watched her eyes. "Maybe spending a couple of weeks in Cancun."

Her eyes opened wide and her face turned scarlet. She lowered her eyes and shook her head furiously. "I've spent my life just trying to be what I really am. I spent the last seven years trying to forget the first thirty. When I had the operation I swore that if I ever met a man I liked I'd never tell him the truth. I couldn't stand to have him look at me like I was a freak."

"You're not. Hey, I don't pretend to understand why you grew up the way you did. I want to know who you are now, not the history."

"But you *know*," she said slowly. "How could you be interested in me?"

"For the same reasons I'm attracted to other women who are smart, and tough, and sexy, and good-looking. No difference."

"I couldn't stand to have someone looking at me and trying to see the past."

"Remember what I said back at the car this morning before I left, when I dropped you off?"

"About how you wanted to see me again after this was over?"

"I meant it."

"You knew then," she said. Her voice was barely audible. "When you said it."

"And everything I said to you last night. Knowing doesn't change anything."

"It's crazy. The odds are so against it."

It was my turn to laugh. It wasn't loud, but it seemed to echo around the quarry. "They always are. You can't let that stop you."

"I don't want a man who's understanding; I want a man who doesn't know in the first place."

"You made quite a speech about accepting yourself a couple of hours ago, and not living a lie."

It was a long time before she answered. "It's been a long-enough day already. And there's a long way to go."

We stood there a moment longer; then the wind picked up and snow started to fall. The water was as still and black as ever. We walked back to the car and drove away.